SPY IN CHANCERY

By the same author

Death of a King
Satan in St. Mary's
Crown in Darkness
The Whyte Harte

SPY IN CHANCERY

P. C. DOHERTY

ST. MARTIN'S PRESS
NEW YORK

 For information, address St. Martin's Press, 175 Fifth Avenue, New York, N.Y. 10010.

Library of Congress Cataloging-in-Publication Data

Doherty, P. C.
Spy in chancery / P.C. Doherty.
p. cm.
ISBN 0-312-02984-5
1. Great Britain—History—Edward I, 1272-1307—Fiction.
I. Title.
PR6054.037S69 1989
823'.914—dc19 89-4086
CIP

First published in Great Britain by Robert Hale Limited.

First U.S. Edition

10 9 8 7 6 5 4 3 2 1

To 'Mother Terrible'
(Grace Fogarty Senior)

ONE

The ship was in no danger despite the storm which raged out of the north to raise the waves and batter the craft. The master, John Ewell, a Southampton burgess and long-time mariner, knew these seas and sensed the temper of the storm. The ship was sturdy enough, two raised poops at either end to allow the archers protection when they fired, the mast was steep but sturdy and a look-out was posted high above the billowing sail just beneath the white red-crossed pennant of England. Ewell had every confidence in his deep-bellied ship and able crew, they were the least of his worries. He paced the deck, ice-blue eyes turned keenly seawards with the odd, sudden glance up to ensure his look-outs were equally attentive, constantly scanning the wind-blasted seas for pursuit.

Ewell congratulated himself. He had been successful, he had managed to slip his ship in and out of the Gascon port without hindrance. A short stay but long enough to pick up the small rolls of parchment sealed in their leather pouch and locked in the iron-bound chest in his narrow cabin. Edward of England would pay well for such reports: gold, special licences, even a knighthood. Despite the icy winds, Ewell hugged his own warmth and desperately wished for the calmer waters of the channel where his ship, the *Saint Christopher*, would find refuge.

Ewell felt exhilarated by what he had achieved. The goddam French may have overrun the English duchy of Gascony, seizing its cities, forts, castles and broken the wine trade between England and Bordeaux but, soon, the tables would be turned. Philip IV of France would kneel in the dust and beg forgiveness of Edward of England. Ewell stopped his pacing and stared into the middle distance, perhaps he would be there when it happened, Edward's captain, a burgess of Southampton, a knight with lands and titles bestowed by a grateful King. Ewell's dreams were suddenly shattered by a cry from the look-out high on the mast.

'Sail! I see sail to the south-east! One, no, two cogs.' Ewell steeled himself and rushed to the rail but could see nothing through the driving rain.

'Where? Where?' he shouted back.

'To the south-east, two cogs, full armaments!'

'What designs do they show?' Ewell yelled back, his throat sore at competing with the wind.

'No colours. Two pennants from the masts!' came the reply.

Ewell hoped they were English. Oh, sweet Christ, he did! No longer the thoughts of land and knighthood but his pleasant-faced wife, young daughters and his beloved ship which strained under the wind. He knew, at the bottom of his heart, that the ships were French, sent in pursuit like greyhounds after a startled hare. Ewell stared around in disbelief, every inch of sail had been loosed to catch the wind, two men on the stern manned the huge tiller, the rest were either below or in the rigging awaiting orders. He turned and saw the white, anxious face of his bo'sun and steward, Stephen Appleby. Ewell checked the panic which clutched his own heart and stomach and tried to put a brave face on it.

'Rouse the men, Stephen,' he said quietly. 'Give them helmets, sallets, cloaks, crossbows and a quiver of quarrels.' Stephen grimaced, nodded and went below, his shouts faint in the roaring wind.

In a while the men stumbled on deck, tired, drawn, white-faced as they fastened their leather jerkins, put on helmets, wrist-guards and desperately tried to keep the cords of their crossbows dry against the cutting rain. Ewell ordered them to their posts on the fighting castles at either end of the ship, as well as into the rigging which ran like snakes up the great central mast. He issued a further spate of orders and two young boys brought sand and salt to strew the slippery docks while another tried to light and heat a small, capped charcoal brazier beneath the mast. Ewell turned back to the rail and peered hopefully through the rain. He saw nothing but, straining his eyes, he suddenly glimpsed dull shapes. The French were upon him. Ewell cursed trying to conceal his panic. Perhaps he could out-run them. But it was early morning and a full day had to elapse before the darkness fell. The English captain knew, at the bottom of his heart, that his ship could not make it. He had no illusions about the French. They had little love for English sailors and the rules of chivalry did not apply to war at sea.

The weather did not break and by noon the French were closing in on them. Two huge cogs, merchantmen converted to war, their great sails had lent them speed, even time to separate so they came in on either side of the English ship. Ewell saw the blue flags adorned with the silver lilies and, more foreboding, beneath them, the Oriflamme pennant which indicated that the French were not taking prisoners. The huge poops of the French were crowded with archers, the decks glistened with massed armour and Ewell saw the faint plume of black smoke which showed that the French had catapults. Ewell looked around in desperation. there was little he could do, surrender was out of the question for, at sea, prisoners were rarely taken. He breathed deeply, prayed to St. Anne and put on his rust-stained breastplate and battered steel helmet. The French closed in on either side, their catapults sending huge, glowing balls of fiery pitch up into the dull grey skies. The first one missed but soon they found their range and a rain of fire fell on the *Saint Christopher*.

The pitch caught the sail, the rigging and woodwork and the tongue of flame licked greedily and grew. The crew made frantic attempts to douse the flames with sand and water but to no avail. Other missiles, huge fiery black clumps caught the sails, turning them into curtains of fire, while the look-outs, trapped in the rigging, screamed and fell in flames to the deck. Ewell shouted at his archers to loose and turned just in time to see one of the French ships crash alongside, its soldiers pouring like a river over its side. The English archers accounted for a few who screamed and twirled as the ugly, jagged crossbow quarrels ripped the flesh of chest and neck, but the French were too many. The second ship also closed, disgorging its troops.

Ewell turned, he would reach his cabin, deny the French that leather, wax-sealed pouch but an arrow caught him full in his exposed throat and he crashed to the deck. He thought he could still move but the blood pumped through his mouth, he saw the blurred faces of his wife, his eldest child and the darkness came crashing down about him. Within an hour the *Saint Christopher* was blazing from the prow to stern. The French ships stood off, their crews watching the bowsprit dip into the waves, its grim burden, the body of the bo'sun, still jerking and twisting. Stephen Appleby died slowly. The noose around his neck strangling off his breath but, just before he died, even in his death agonies, he wondered, once again, how the French had known and found his ship.

* * *

In the rue Barbette in Paris, Nicholas Poer hunched over his bowl of rancid meat, leeks and onions, slurping from the horn spoon he always carried with him. He stared round the dirty tavern, slyly studying the other customers sitting on up-turned barrels of broken stools. The place was poorly lighted by thick tallow candles which gave off a putrid smell. Poer did not like it, he heard a rat rustle the dirty straw which covered the earth-packed floor and turned back to his food, wondering what he was really eating. He raised the battered pewter tankard and drained its contents, the raw beer stinging the sores in his mouth. He felt frightened, almost shaking with panic though he tried to conceal it, drawing comfort from the long dagger he clutched under his cloak.

Of Gascon parents, Poer spoke fluent French and knew Paris well. He had always been confident in his disguise, no one would suspect that this greasy-haired, shabby, unshaven individual was a trained clerk of the Royal Exchequer of England, Edward I's highly trained spy sent to Paris to collect and send back information. Poer had moved easily around the city, crossing skilfully from the underworld on the left bank of the Seine to the slovenly splendour of the royal household in the Louvre. Poer had, in recent weeks, been excited by what he had discovered. The French king, together with his brothers, Charles and Louis, was planning another move against Edward of England. Something breathtaking, a Grand Design, so an usher of the court had assured him when deep in his cups: Poer believed he had to discover what it was yet recently he had become afraid.

He was certain he was being watched, trailed as he

made his way down the alleys and runnels of Paris. Earlier in the day he had been in the great square before the Cathedral of Notre Dame, watching a mountebank eat fire while his sons juggled with coloured baubles and there, Poer experienced the same feeling of dread which had assailed him a few days earlier. Someone was following him and though he had turned and twisted, never once did he catch a glimpse of the malicious watching eyes. This evening, as he made his way back to his lodgings in the garret of a mercer's house, Poer's disquiet had grown; the gentle slither of leather over wet cobbles, shadows deep in doorways, the soft clip-clop of a trained war-horse but, when he looked, there was nothing.

Poer finished his meal and slowly gazed round the dingy tavern room, he had sought sanctuary here, hoping his pursuers would show themselves, but he had been disappointed. Only an old beggar, his legs cut off at the knees, had hobbled in, the wooden slats fixed to his hands and the stumps of his legs clattering like drum-beats on the tavern floor. He watched the man eat like a dog lapping its bowl and scrabble out as Poer rose, wrapped his cloak about him and slipped out into the icy streets. Poer turned and made his way down the narrow alley, the timber and wattle houses stretching high above him, each tier jutting out above the other so the roofs of the houses closed in like conspirators locking out the frozen sky.

Poer stared up, the windows and doors were tightly shuttered, no sound except the moaning of the wind which rolled the mist and battered, almost with malicious glee, some loosened shutter. Poer drew his dagger and walked down the centre of the street, keeping clear of the dirt and ordure piled outside each door as well as the rank, fetid sewer which ran down the middle. He saw a shadow move in one of the doorways and a white, skeletal arm shot out, followed by the whine of a beggar.

'Ah, Monsieur, *ayez pitié, ayez pitié.*' Poer showed his long cruel dagger, the man disappeared and the beggar's voice faded.

Poer walked on cautiously. There was something wrong, something which had just happened but he could not place it. He was too tired, too anxious. He did not want to be arrested as a spy, to be dragged on a hurdle to the gallows at Montfauçon, strapped to a wheel and whirled naked whilst red-hooded executioners carefully broke each of his limbs with their wicked, jagged iron bars. Poer shivered and, holding his dagger before him, left the alleyway. He felt better now. He was at the crossroads, massive lighted braziers were placed here every evening by the civic authorities and a huge tallow candle fixed in the niche before the statue of the saint of that particular quarter, such light and heat drove off the icy mist and reassured Poer.

He whirled to his left as he heard the clack of wood on stone but only the old beggar from the tavern came out of the mist, whining and dragging himself across the cobbles in front of Poer. The spy ignored him and started to cross the square, the clatter increased in speed and Poer suddenly realised what was wrong, the old man had left a few seconds before him yet he had reached the top of the alleyway. Poer hesitated, turned but it was too late, the old man hurled into him, trapping his legs and Poer, stumbling over him, his hands caught in the folds of his cloak, fell, a sickening thud as his head hit the sharp cobbles.

The 'old beggar' pulled himself clear, his hands scrabbling behind him as he loosened the straps which pulled back his legs, the wooden slats were jerked from his knees and he straightened up. One glance at the fallen man showed there was no need to hurry, his victim was still unconscious. The beggar whistled quietly and was answered by the clip-clop of a great black war-horse which came out of the mist like some phantom from the gates of hell. Its rider, muffled in a dark cloak and hood, dismounted and walked over to the prostrate man, others joined him out of the darkness to form a threatening circle round the unconscious body.

'Is he dead?' the rider asked, his voice dry, devoid of any emotion.

'No,' the beggar muttered. 'Only unconscious. Is he to be questioned?' The leader shook his head and gathered the reins of his horse.

'No,' he replied. 'Sew him in a sack and throw him into the Seine!'

'It would be a mercy to cut his throat,' the beggar pointed out. The leader mounted and savagely jerked at the reins to turn his horse.

'Mercy!' he commented drily. 'If you had failed or lost him, I would have shown you such a mercy. He is a spy! He deserves none. Do as I say!' He turned, and soon both horse and rider were hidden by the cloying mist.

TWO

Edward, King of England and Duke of Aquitaine, was furious. In the council chamber near the royal chapel at Westminster, he was indulging in one of his passionate regal rages. Swathed in robes, his council sat and meekly witnessed the royal drama, some closely studied the red-gold tapestries covering the whitewashed walls, others scuffed their boots in the rush-strewn floor trying to rub the cold numbness from their legs and feet. It was cold, freezing, despite the large, iron charcoal braziers which had been wheeled into the room. The wind battered the shutters on the horn-glazed windows, piercing the cracks and blowing cold blasts of air to waft and fan the flames of the candles and the oil in their sconce stones. The clerks sat, pens poised above the thick, silk-smooth parchment, they realised the King did not want his curses transcribed so they patiently waited, hoping their fingers would not lose their feeling or the ink freeze in their metal pots.

Edward had no such reservations, time and again, he brought his fists crashing down on the long wooden table.

'My Lords,' he bellowed. 'There is treason here, rank and foul as the contents of any sewer!'

'Your Grace,' Robert Winchelsea, Archbishop of

Canterbury, intervened quickly, hoping to calm the King. 'It would seem ...'

'It would seem,' Edward harshly interrupted, 'My Lord of Canterbury, that the royal arse cannot fart without Philip IV of France knowing it!'

Winchelsea nodded, fully agreeing with the sentiment, though not with Edward's unique way of expressing it. The archbishop decided to remain silent, Edward's rages were becoming more frequent, the deaths of the beloved Queen Eleanor, his Chancellor and friend, Robert Burnell, Bishop of Bath and Wells, had loosened dark forces in the King's soul. His blond hair and beard were streaked with white, that once bronzed skin now sallow and pulled in deep lines around the sharp blue eyes and thin-lipped mouth.

Winchelsea sipped from the cup of mulled wine and scowled, it had gone cold, the archbishop leaned back in his chair and heartily wished the King's anger would cool as quickly as his wine. At last the King quietened, he sat upright in his great, oak-carved chair at the top of the table, his be-ringed hands twisted into fists.

'My Lords,' he said slowly, drawing deep gulps of air. 'There is a traitor amongst us.' He jabbed at the table top. 'Here in Westminster, a traitor, a spy who tells the French everything, our secrets, our plans, our designs. The *Saint Christopher* has undoubtedly been caught and sunk and one of our most valuable spies, a man many of you know well, a high-ranking clerk in the Exchequer, Nicholas Poer, has been murdered in Paris.' Edward stopped and the council stirred itself, there were exclamations, groans, mutters and curses. 'Poer,' Edward continued, 'was taken out of the Seine. He had been stitched alive into a sack and drowned like an unwanted cat. Someone, someone here might have informed the French about him for Poer was too clever to let slip his disguise and be caught. The same is true of the *Saint Christopher*. Philip IV, God damn him, must have been informed of its mission to collect reports from our spies in Gascony. God only knows what has happened to them!'

Edward stared dully around the chamber, a pretence while he plotted his words and studied the faces of his councillors. One of them was a traitor. But who? Robert Winchelsea, his sainted Archbishop of Canterbury? A prelate of the church? Edward did not trust the man, an upstart, a sanctimonious clerk, a shallow man who always supported noble causes. On the King's left, Edmund, Earl of Lancaster. Edward stared at his brother's thin white face framed by long, black hair. He felt a touch of compassion whenever he studied his brother. Edmund had always been sickly and looked permanently ill with his slightly withered arm and cruel, distorted right shoulder. An accident at birth, or so they said. Yet, Edward had heard the stories about Edmund really being the first born, Henry III's eldest son but overlooked because of his disabilities, the crown passing to his stronger, more acceptable brother? Lies! Edward knew the truth but often wondered if his brother did. Edmund had been in charge of Gascony yet he had quietly surrendered it to the French, tricked, outmanoeuvred, making his name and the crown of England a laughing-stock in Europe.

Edward's gaze passed on. Next to Edmund sat John of Brittany, Earl of Richmond. Another fool, Edward thought. Richmond held lands in France and was related, albeit tenuously, to Philip IV. Edward often wondered if Richmond had been bought for a price, a little higher than the usual thirty pieces of silver. Edward silently ground his teeth. He had trusted that florid-faced fool as a son. For what? Richmond had taken an expeditionary force to France, invaded Gascony and promptly surrendered. Edward looked around. There were others, Bohun, Earl of Hereford, and Bigod, Earl of Norfolk. God's teeth, a precious pair!

Oh, he knew them, how they resented his attempts to control the power of the great nobles and exploited his present difficulties with Scotland and France to their own profit and gain. Really, Edward thought, he did not mind that, he'd been playing such a game for decades. But treason? Well, Edward thought, that was a different matter, their heads would roll and bodies split open as easy as any other. Yet, he would have to catch them, send them to the scaffold on hard, indisputable evidence. His judges would demand that, evidence, not hearsay of treason.

Edward stared at the clerks, even they, his own creatures, men of peasant stock, who had bettered themselves by luck, intellect and royal favour, were not above examination. Edward glanced suspiciously at one of them, Ralph Waterton, a dark-haired, handsome youth with smiling eyes and a ready wit. Waterton was a good clerk but Edward's spies had reported that Waterton lived above his station, enjoying luxuries no chancery clerk could really afford. And what happens if the spies themselves had been suborned? Could they be trusted? *Quis custodiet custodes?'* as Augustine had said, 'Who would guard the guards?' Edward's tired mind turned and whirled like some silly mongrel chasing his tail. He suddenly realised the room was deathly quiet. His councillors, clerks and noblemen staring strangely at him. Edward did not want the pretence to continue.

'My Lords,' he smiled, hiding his own secret fears and doubts, 'there must be a resolution to these difficulties when we meet again.' The King turned to Waterton. 'Ralph,' he said kindly. 'Tell Sir Thomas the council is finished and arrange barges to be brought to the palace quay.' Waterton rose and the council meeting broke up, the individual lords and high-ranking applicants made their obeisances, gladly leaving the suspicious atmosphere of the royal presence.

The chamber soon emptied, the King being left to his gloomy thoughts. A gentle tap on the door and Sir Thomas Tuberville, knight banneret of the royal household and captain of the guard, pushed his way silently into the room.

'Sir Thomas?' the King liked this man, a fierce fighter despite his long, white face and sharp, green eyes which constantly regarded the world in an anxious, fearful manner.

'Sire,' the knight replied, 'the lords of the council have left. Is there anything else you want?'

'No, Thomas,' the King gently replied. 'There is nothing. Stand guard. Do not dismiss the men. I shall be a while yet.' The knight bowed and left, quietly closing the door behind him.

The King rose and went across to warm his frozen fingers over one of the braziers. Deep in his heart, the King was worried; Eleanor, his beautiful Spanish madonna of a queen was dead; Burnell, his wily old chancellor likewise, and the King felt a crushing sense of loss. He was alone, trusting nobody at a time he needed someone to trust; Scotland was ablaze with rebellion, his secret plans to bring it under the jurisdiction of the English crown ruined by Scottish lords determined to have their own king, even the Devil himself, rather than accept a royal writ from Westminster. Gascony, England's rich province in south-western France, was also gone, taken in a month by trickery and deceit.

Philip IV, King of France, grandson of the sainted Louis XI, Edward ruefully reflected, was a prince of liars who would win the admiration of Beelzebub, the king of liars. Edward moaned aloud at the way he had been duped; a border incident concerning certain castles on the Franco-Gascon boundary, Philip, technically Edward's overlord in the matter of the Duchy of

Gascony, had demanded that the province be handed over to him for thirty days while the dispute was settled. Edward ground his teeth at what happened next. His own dear brother, Edmund, had agreed, later justifying his actions by all sorts of legal nonsense. The French had immediately occupied it and Philip IV, that white-faced, devious bastard, had refused to cede it back. His troops poured into the duchy like a river breaking a dam, and all was lost.

Edward had complained bitterly to Philip, the Pope and other princes of Europe. Oh, they had been sorry. They thought it was a terrible violation of a vassal's feudal rights but Edward knew they would not help, behind their polite diplomatic statements, they were laughing at him. Yet this had only been the beginning of the nightmare; Edward's spies began to send in reports of a secret, grand design by Philip to isolate England, striking through Scotland, Wales, Ireland and Gascony. Edward had brought Wales firmly under his control, Scotland could be subjected and Gascony regained, but what if the reverse was true? If Philip took all these provinces before launching an all-out assault on England. Duke William of Normandy had done the same two hundred years before.

Edward's own grandfather, John, had lost all of England's possessions in northern France and had to face a French invasion of England. Was the pattern going to repeat itself? Edward frowned and cracked his knuckles. He had made a serious mistake, he had underestimated Philip IV, nicknamed 'Le Bel', the French King had fooled everyone with his coy, blond looks, frank blue eyes and honest, down-to-earth approach. Now Edward knew better. Philip was intent on creating an empire which would have made Charlemagne gasp in amazement.

Edward flexed his fingers above the brazier. There

must be a way out, he thought; he would reinforce the Welsh garrisons and send an army north to smash the Scots. And Philip IV? Edward sighed. He would grovel to the Pope, kiss his satin sandal, place England and its territories under his protection. Grandfather John had done the same with brilliant results. If anybody attacked England, they would, in fact, be assaulting the Holy Father and all the might of the Catholic Church. Edward grinned, he would send bushels of gold to that old reprobate, Pope Boniface VIII, and ask him to intervene, arbitrate. At the same time, he would root out the traitors here in Westminster. But whom could he trust? Whom would Burnell have chosen? Edward thought and his grin almost broke into a laugh. Of course! The King of England had chosen his man.

* * *

Hugh Corbett, senior clerk in the royal chancery of England, knelt before the statue of the Virgin in the palatial, incense-smelling lady chapel of the Cathedral of Notre Dame in Boulogne-sur-Mer. The English clerk was not a religious man but he believed that the good Christ and his mother should be treated with every courtesy, so he prayed when he remembered to. Corbett found prayer hard, he did most of the talking while God always seemed too busy to answer him. Corbett had lit a pure beeswax candle and now knelt in its circle of light, desperately trying to fulfil his vow.

He had made it during that God-forsaken voyage from England in a squat, fat-bellied cog which seemed to have a will of its own, almost malicious in the damage it had caused. On leaving Dover, it had run into a storm and backed and heaved itself across the swelling sullen waves. An icy, blasting wind had filled the sail, tossing the ship like a leaf on a pond and

Corbett had spent the entire voyage crouched in the bows, vomiting and retching till he thought his heart would give out.

The cold sea water poured through the scuppers, soaking his already freezing body until Corbett thought he was going to die. He could not move for what was the use? Only to vomit and be despatched back to the rail by his equally discomforted colleagues. Corbett's only consolation was that his body-servant, Ranulf, had been as ill. Usually a man of robust appetites, Ranulf had joined his master in his agony. Corbett had, at last, taken a vow, promising to light a candle in the Cathedral Church of Notre Dame and kneel in an hour's prayer in the Lady Chapel, if the Virgin brought him safely to shore.

Corbett had found lighting the candle an easy task but the hour's prayer had turned into a careful analysis of why the King had sent him to France in the first place. Corbett sighed, rose from his knees and leaned against one of the pillars, staring down into the darkness of the nave. He was a senior clerk in the chancery now, responsible for letters, memoranda, indentures, warrants and other documents issued under the secret seal of England, responsible only to the Chief Justiciar, Chancellor and King of England. A secure, well-paid job with fat fees and the right to draw on supplies from the King's own household, he had his own small house off Holborn, monies deposited with a goldsmith and even more with a Sienese banker.

Corbett had few ties, no wife, no child, and he had reached his thirty-eighth year still enjoying robust health in an age when a man was lucky to pass his thirty-fifth. Corbett slid down and crouched at the base of the huge, fluted pillar. His stomach was still unsettled and he felt weak and unsteady from the sea crossing. Corbett cursed, he was back on his travels again, entrusted once more with secret and delicate tasks. He had thought that all was over now when his master, Burnell, had died some four years ago. Old Burnell, cunning, saintly with a streak of devious genius in rooting out any threat to the realm. Now he was gone, Corbett had been a member of the bodywatch which had knelt and prayed over the old bishop's stiffening corpse before it was shrouded and laid to rest in its pinewood coffin.

Since his old master's death, Corbett's life had flowed and ebbed like some sluggish stream until the King intervened and summoned him to a secret meeting at his palace of Eltham. The King was planning a fresh expedition against the Scots and the room had been full of trunks, cases and leather chancery pouches containing letters, memoranda and bills concerning the Scottish question. Edward had quickly come to the point: there was a traitor or traitors in his own chancery or on his council who were collecting vital secret information on England's affairs and passing it, God knows how the King fumed, to Philip IV of France. Corbett was to be an envoy, join an embassy to the French court and discover the traitor.

'Be on your guard,' the King bleakly commented, 'the traitor could well be one of your companions. You are to find him, Master Corbett, trap him in his filth!'

'Shall I arrest him, your Grace?'

'If possible,' came the bland reply, 'but, if that is not feasible, kill him!'

Corbett shuddered and stared round the quiet, sombre church. He had come to pray and yet plotted death. He heard a sound at the back of the church and wearily rose. Ranulf would be waiting for him: the English clerk genuflected towards the solitary flickering sanctuary lamp and walked slowly down the nave.

Corbett breathed deeply, slowly, he wished to remain calm, even though he was certain there was someone in the church, lurking in the darkness, watching him.

THREE

The day after Corbett's visit to Notre Dame, the English envoys had sufficiently recovered from the ordeal at sea to begin their journey, following the coast down to the Somme before turning south to Paris. They had brought their own horses and baggage across, a cumbersome trail of animals carrying supplies for my lords the Earls of Richmond and Lancaster, not to mention the clerks, scribes, cooks, cursors, bailiffs, priests and doctors. There was no obvious distinction in degree or status, the biting cold weather and shrill, sharp winds ensured everyone was wrapped in thick brown cloaks.

Now there was the usual chaos outside the small monastery they had lodged in after leaving the port, horses were saddled, two needed a farrier, one was lame, another had sores on its back; girths, bridles and stirrups were checked, broken or damaged ones repaired before clothing, manuscripts and other baggage were loaded noisily on to them alongside provisions purchased at exorbitant prices from sly-eyed merchants. The calm of the monastery courtyard was shattered by cries, shouted orders, curses and the angry neighs of nervous, highly-strung horses. A number of mongrels wandered in to share and spread the confusion, only to be chased away by an irate, stick-wielding lay brother.

Corbett sat on a ruined bench in the corner of the courtyard and morosely watched the chaos. The shouts and curses would have drowned the cries of the damned in hell; Corbett stared up at the huge tympanum carved above the monastery church door where, etched eternally in stone, the damned hanged by their bellies from trees of fire while more smothered in furnaces, their hands across their mouths, their stone eyes staring through plumes of smoke; Christ in judgement held the saved in his hands while the wicked were swallowed by monstrous fish, some gnawed by demons, tormented by serpents, fire, ice or tormented by fruits forever hanging out of reach of their starving maws. Corbett morosely concluded such terrors were nothing compared to the experience of being sent across the channel in freezing winter on an English embassy to France.

'Master Corbett,' the clerk groaned and got up as his servant, Ranulf, shoved his way through the crowded courtyard, the man's red hair glowing like a beacon above his white, anxious face. Corbett had saved Ranulf from the gallows some ten years before, now he was the clerk's faithful steward and companion, at least superficially, for Corbett knew Ranulf *atte* Newgate had a powerful interest in bettering himself at the expense of everyone else, Corbett included. Ranulf could lie, cheat and betray with a skill which constantly astonished and amused the clerk while Ranulf's pursuit of other men's wives would, Corbett privately maintained, bring his servant to a violent and sudden end.

Now, Ranulf was acting the role of the agitated, concerned servant, slyly hoping he could disturb his secretive, solemn master.

'It's Blaskett!' Ranulf said breathlessly. 'He says we are ready to leave soon and asks if your baggage is packed and loaded?' Blaskett was the pompous, arrogant peacock of a steward in the Earl of Lancaster's household. A man who loved authority and all its show like other men loved gold.

'Is our baggage loaded, Ranulf?' Corbett asked.

'Yes.'

'And are we ready to leave?'

'Yes.'

'Then why not tell my lord Blaskett!' Ranulf stared like a man who had just received a great secret, nodded and, turning on his heel, bustled back into the monastery to continue his malicious baiting of the pigeon-breasted Blaskett.

The English embassy departed just as the monastery bells were booming out for Terce; the French escort were waiting for them outside the monastery gate, a pursuivant of Philip's court, resplendent in scarlet and black, three nondescript clerks and two knights in half-armour, their sleeveless jerkins covering breastplates displaying the blue and gold of the royal French household. They were accompanied by a number of mounted men-at-arms, rough looking veterans, wearing boiled leather jerkins, steel breastplates and thick woollen serge leggings pushed into stout riding-boots. Corbett watched Lancaster and Richmond talk to the knights, documents were exchanged and, with the mounted escort strung out on either side of them, the English embassy continued its journey.

The Normandy countryside was flat, brown and still in the mailed fist of winter. Some hardy peasants, their russet cloaks belted around them, felt hats pulled over their eyes, attempted to break the ground for sowing: behind them, their families, women, even small children worked scattering marle, lime or manure to fertilise the soil. To Corbett, who had witnessed the ravages of war on the marcher counties during King Edward's Welsh wars, the land seemed prosperous enough. Nevertheless, he remembered the saying of Jacques of Vitry, 'what the peasant gains by stubborn work in a year, the lord will devour in an hour'. Justice was harsh, the lords of the manor in their walled, moated homes of wood and stone, exercised more justice than they did in England and every crossroad had its scaffold or stocks.

The villages were a collection of cottages, each with a small garden surrounded by a hedge and shallow ditch but Corbett was particularly struck by the number of towns, some old but others only in existence for decades; each was walled, the houses clustered around an abbey, cathedral or church. Sometimes the English stayed in one of these places, such as Noyon and Beauvis, where there was a welcoming priory or tavern spacious enough to host them. On other occasions, a variety of manors, royal or otherwise, were compelled to accept them. The French knights would flaunt their warrants, demanding purveyance which obliged the hapless lord or steward to feed the envoys and their entourage. Nevertheless, despite such hospitality, Corbett and his colleagues were left well alone by their French escort who treated them in a sullen, off-hand manner. On reflection, Corbett was not surprised, a state of armed truce existed between France and England with every indication that both countries might soon slip into war.

Corbett soon tired of the endless, daily tasks and problems of travelling though men like Blaskett thrived on them. The little things, the chatter, the gossip, who sat where, who was due what monies, it sounded glorious to be sent on an embassy to France: Corbett knew many of his colleagues would seize and enhance such an opportunity, forgetting the sores on their arses and thighs from constant riding, the rat-infested hostels, the rancid meat and sour wine which turned their bowels to water and the journey into a nightmare. The company of the great was no consolation, Lancaster was mean, sour-mouthed and taciturn: Brittany was conscious of his own importance, was eager to forget his recent military expedition to Gascony which had made him the laughing stock of the English court. The clerk, Waterton, seemed an amiable fellow, but he kept to himself except where women were concerned, almost rivalling Ranulf in sexual prowess. Corbett often heard the sounds of revelry at night, the slap of hand on some wench's soft bottom, the giggles, screams and cries of lovemaking.

At the same time, beneath the banality of this tedious journey, Corbett felt there was distrust and tension. Once they left Boulogne, Corbett lost his sense of being watched but he did experience the lack of trust betwen the leaders of the English embassy. King Edward had told Corbett that Lancaster, Brittany and Waterton, as well as the young, taciturn Henry Eastry, a monk of Canterbury and notary to Archbishop Winchelsea, were all privy to the secret business to Edward's council, anyone of them could be the traitor betraying information and English lives to the French.

Corbett quietly watched Eastry, Waterton and the two earls, but they did nothing unusual, regarding the French with the same studied dislike as the rest of the entourage. None of them had any contact more than they should have with their escort or made any effort, even secretly, to communicate with any French official in the towns they passed through.

It took two weeks to reach the outskirts of Paris after the most banal and boring journey in Corbett's life. The clerk felt stifled by the grinding routine but, looking back, realised that made it the ideal time for an ambush. They were on the Beauvais road, a broad, rutted track which swept into Paris, bordered by thick clumps of trees when the attackers struck; dressed in black, red hoods over their faces, they thundered from the trees and swooped down on the English party. The French escort turned, their leaders drawing swords and crying out orders just as the assailants crashed into them.

Corbett, grasping his long dagger, lashed out furiously, turning his horse, terrified lest one of the attackers got behind him for a quick, easy slash to the back of his neck. He sensed he was in the thick of the fight, frightened by the terrifying horsemen pushing through towards him and wondered why the assailants had chosen this point of the column and not its head where Lancaster and Richmond rode, or the rear where the baggage carts carried possible plunder. A figure loomed up before him, cloak flapping, eyes glistening with malice through the eye-holes of the hood, arm raised to drive the mace down for the killing blow. Corbett threw himself along his horse's neck, lunging with his dagger at his assailant's exposed belly, but the man wore hard armour beneath his cloak. Corbett felt the blade jar and a streak of pain ran up his arm. Nevertheless, the blow forced his opponent to drop his club and turn away clutching his stomach.

Corbett, the sweat now soaking his body, whirled in terror, he was surrounded by attackers though the rest of the English entourage were beginning to assert themselves and Corbett could see the French escort, rather dilatory at first, were making their presence felt. There were screams, curses, men fell, choking in the saddle, blood pumping from open wounds; axes, daggers and clubs whirled and Corbett heard the chilling whine of a jagged crossbow bolt. Ranulf came up beside him, blood streaming from a cut on his face, eyes staring madly, a white froth on his lips. He screamed soundlessly but Corbett ignored him as he glanced wildly around, eyes darting, looking to see if the crossbow man was friendly or hostile. Then, as sudden as their attack came, the assailants drew off, thundering back across the field in a cloud of dust.

Corbett sat, slumped over his horse, fighting back the nausea which threatened to disgrace him. He stopped the sobbing in his throat and looked around; there were bodies sprawled on the road, men screaming and cursing at the rawness of their wounds. The long column was now broken: two horses lay dead, another kicked in its traces, blood streaming from its throat. Gradually order was restored. There were a number of dead, two soldiers, a scullion in the Duke of Richmond's household and one of the attackers. Corbett watched Lancaster and Richmond scream aloud about 'Outlaws, so near to Paris,' ' Lack of protection,' but the knights shrugged and, shoulders raised, deprecatingly asked if there were no outlaws in England?

Lancaster intervened and called a meeting of his colleagues, Richmond, Waterton, Eastry and Corbett. They watched from the road while the serjeants and stewards resorted order, the physician tended wounds while the French knights went off to commandeer a cart to take the dead and seriously wounded to a nearby manor. Richmond looked flushed, keen to brag about his own sword play, Waterton looked nervous, unmarked, not even a stain or cut, Eastry was sorrowful but coldy detached, eager to get back and give solace to the wounded, Lancaster looked furious, his white face mottled with anger.

'Of course,' the earl began, 'I will personally protest at this attack to Philip IV. What we have to decide,' he patted his horse's neck and looked round the group, 'is whether it was an outlaw assault or a carefully planned attack. I think it was the latter.' A murmur of agreement broke out so Lancaster pressed his point.

'If so,' his voice dropped to a hoarse whisper, 'the

traitor must be amongst us.'

'Why?' Corbett abruptly asked. 'I mean, my Lord, our route was planned in England and, due to the noise our cavalcade makes, half of Normandy must be aware of us.'

Lancaster's eyes slid back to the quiet, reserved clerk. He did not like Corbett, too guarded, the earl thought, too sure of himself. Corbett saw the flicker of dislike in Lancaster's eyes and stifled further questions. The English clerk did not agree with the earl's conclusion, the traitor may well be amongst them but wild, vague accusations would make everyone guarded, cautious and so make discovery of the truth all the more difficult. The earl himself realised this.

'I think,' he continued, 'the traitor is with us, but when we arrive in Paris, we will contact Simon Fauvel, one of the King's agents there. He may have heard some chatter or gossip which could shed some light on these mysteries.'

The group then returned to the now organised column and recommenced its slow journey into the outer suburbs of Paris. Corbett took his place, telling an anxious Ranulf that he was well, safe and unwounded and would appreciate it if his servant shut his mouth and left him alone. Ranulf drew back, muttering angrily while Corbett mulled over the attack. He had heard one of the French escort shout that those assailants who had been killed could not be identified, they carried no documents nor wore any emblem or device. Corbett expected that: the attack was planned but what really worried him was why the brunt of the attack seemed to be aimed at him. Why, he wondered, did someone believe he was so dangerous that he should be singled out for such a dangerous attack? Who in England had passed such information to the French? Corbett pulled his cloak around him, he felt cold, more from fear than the chill, biting wind.

* * *

The fierce biting wind made the horsemen huddle closer to their mounts as they tried to get protection against the cold gusts whistling through the ruined windows and crumbling walls of the ancient church. Their leader, a Breton mercenary, cursed and stamped his feet on the ground in an attempt to recover some warmth. He was also angry at the failure of his attack and did not relish the coming meeting with Monsieur de Craon, Philip IV's chief clerk and master spy, who was now picking his way across the ruins to meet him. To the Breton's superstitious mind the French clerk, small and dark, in his thick black woollen cloak seemed a fiend out of hell. The Breton was usually afraid of no man but Monsier de Craon exuded power as a woman did perfume and did not understand failure or opposition.

De Craon pulled back the cowl of his cloak and went close up to the Breton totally ignoring the mercenary's vast bulk towering above him.

'You launched the attack?' the clerk's voice was soft and polite.

'Yes, we did.'

'And you killed the man?'

The Breton shook his head. 'No, we did not,' he replied and stepped back at the sudden look of hatred in de Craon's eyes. De Craon seemed to be on the verge of losing his temper. He spun on his heel and walked a few paces away before coming back, the only sign of his anger being the constant biting of his lower lip. He brought six bags of gold from beneath his robe.

'These,' he rasped, 'would have been yours if the man had been killed.' De Craon took one of the bags between his finger and thumb, stared coolly at the Breton and dropped the bag at the soldier's feet. 'But you failed and so you only get one.' De Craon strode away, beneath his robe he clenched the bags of gold coins tightly so they bit into his hands but the Frenchman ignored the pain. He had wanted Corbett dead. He hated the man for being what he was as well as what he might do. De Craon stopped for a while and stared around the ruined chancel of the church he had met the assassins in, then he smiled, there would be other occasions to settle past debts with Monsieur Corbett.

FOUR

In Paris, Simon Fauvel, Edward I's agent to the French Court, was on his knees in a small church in the student quarter of the left bank of the Seine. Fauvel liked the tiny, close, musty church; its stark, bare walls and simple lines gave it an aura of purity, a place of prayer untouched by the glitter and gaudy colours of the outside world. Fauvel was not so much a religious man but a cynic tired of the mystery and intrigue which swirled through his normal life; the pretence, the deception, the clever words and phrases which disguised greed, power and the lust to rule. Fauvel knew all about these; as one of King Edward's agents at the French court, he kept the English king informed of developments, attempting to sift the kernel of truth from the thick dross of lies.

'A Peritus' or lawyer on Gascon affairs, Fauvel's task was to argue with French officials and lawyers ever eager to extend Philip's rights over the duchy. Now, Fauvel wearily thought, Philip IV had the duchy and seemed reluctant to give it back. Of course, Fauvel had protested but the French had just shrugged and murmured that such problems could not be solved in a day.

Fauvel tried to clear his mind and concentrate on the reason for visiting the church. It was the anniversary of his wife's death and, every year, he always set aside an hour to pray for her soul, the same date, the same hour when her breath had stopped rattling in her throat and she died of the fever, alone, except for a hedge priest, for Fauvel had been absent on the King's business in France. Fauvel had never really forgiven himself and vowed that on the anniversary of the date and time of her death as well as his neglect of her, God would see him on his knees in prayer. Fauvel scratched his balding head, grimacing at the cold seeping through his knees and thighs from the icy paving stones and tried to ignore the distraction of what he had so recently discovered. There was a traitor in England, the French were well informed about Edward's councils, as they were about their own designs and plots. Fauvel had chosen not to write to Edward about his anxieties but hoped the English embassy under King Edward's brother, the Earl of Lancaster, would soon reach Paris. Fauvel sighed.

He could not pray and soon the bells of Notre Dame would be tolling Vespers, a time of public worship as well as the signal for the beginning of the curfew. Fauvel got up, stretched and tried to rub the cold out of his thighs. Paris was dangerous at night and he was already anxious about Nicholas Poer, the spy from the English chancery whose regular meetings with him had so abruptly ceased. Was Poer alive or dead? Fauvel wondered. He shrugged to himself, such problems would have to wait until Lancaster arrived.

Fauvel pulled the hood close about his face, eyed the deserted, eerie church and stepped into the narrow, dark street. There were still a few people about but he hurried along, eager to reach his lodgings. A beggar rushed out of the shadows, whining for alms, Fauvel pushed him away but the fellow followed, tugging at his cloak and screeching for a sou. Fauvel turned cursing but the beggar persisted, following him like a tormented demon, loudly protesting and shouting abuse. At last, just outside his lodgings, Fauvel exasperated, stopped, turned and dug into his purse.

'Take these and be off!' The beggar grasped Fauvel's wrist, its warmth and strength surprised the cautious English agent, he should have known better but it was too late for as he began to slip backwards, the beggar suddenly lunged forward and drove the dagger, concealed in his other hand, straight into Fauvel's throat.

* * *

Corbett shouldered his way through the busy, gaudy-smelling throng. He had been in Paris seven days and was trying to forget his own problems by visiting the self-proclaimed capital of Europe. Paris stretched from the Grands Boulevards on the right bank of the Seine to the Luxembourg Gardens on the left, the city had grown round the castles and manor houses of the King and was spreading out to include the great homes of the merchant princes as well as the wood and daub houses of the artisans.

The city of Paris was centred on the Île de la Cité in the Seine on which stood the Cathedral of Notre Dame, the Hôtel Dieu and the Royal Palace of the Louvre. Paris was ruled by its kings but dominated by its guilds: each trade had its own quarter; the apothecaries in the city: the literary trades, parchment sellers, scribes, illuminators, booksellers in the Latin quarter on the left bank of the Seine: money-changers, Jews, Lombards and goldsmiths on the Grand Port. As he neared the Grand Châtelet, Corbett noted that the trades, forbidden to tout their wares, displayed huge signs, a giant glove, pestle or hat.

Paris was a prosperous city with busy markets: bread in the Place Maribet: meat in the Grand Châtelet: St. Germain for sausages: flowers and geegaws on the Petit Port. Corbett wandered down the great boulevard which would allow two or three carts abreast to the Great Orberie or herb market on the quayside opposite the Île de la Cité. Corbett loved the sweet crushed smell of herbs which reminded him of his native west Sussex and, though a shy man, he also loved crowds and the sharp, devious manner of the merchants when doing business. Corbett wandered amongst the stalls trying to detect which butchers bled out the meat or used the blood to freshen the gills of old, stale fish. He was fascinated by deception, the way things could be made to appear in sharp contrast with the way they really were.

Politics were no different, Corbett had been surprised by what had happened since his arrival in Paris and he needed time to think, reflect and analyse. The English envoys had been given a large manor house near the main Paris bridge across the Seine, a large rambling affair with crenellated walls, spiked towers and a huge courtyard. The English soon made themselves at home, men like Blaskett had their virtues for their love of power meant order was soon imposed, supplies bought, kitchens cleaned and ready for use. On the third day of their arrival in Paris, the principal English envoys were invited to meet King Philip and his council in the Louvre Palace on the Île de la Cité. They had assembled in its large hall, decked with blazing blood-red banners, exquisite drapes and the blue and gold colours of the royal household.

Fresh rushes sprinkled with spring flowers had been strewn on the floor and a host of great iron candelabra burning beeswax candles were placed around the heavy, oaken table on the dais at the far end of the hall.

Lancaster, Corbett and the other English envoys sat at one side of this and rose suddenly when trumpets brayed and King Philip with his entourage swept into the room. Corbett was immediately struck by the majesty of the French king dressed from head to toe in a blue velvet gown trimmed with snow-white costly ermine, the gown being decorated with silver fleur-de-lis and gathered close by a thick gold belt. The King's blond hair, bound by a silver coronet, fell down to his shoulders to frame a white face, narrow eyes, a beak of a nose and thin bloodless lips.

Philip IV, exuding majesty in his every gesture, had nodded at Lancaster before sitting down in a great oaken chair at the head of the table and, with a weary wave of a purple-gloved hand, gestured to the English envoys and members of his own entourage to take their seats. Corbett did, almost standing up again in surprise when he noticed the small, dark figure beside the French king; the man was glaring at him, not bothering to hide the malice glistening in his eyes. Corbett looked again in disbelief but there was no mistaking Amaury de Craon, special envoy of the French crown. Corbett had encountered him in Scotland some years earlier and, judging by the malice in de Craon's stare, the French clerk had not forgiven nor forgotten the way Corbett had outwitted him. Corbett glanced away, gathered his thoughts and hid his surprise beneath an inscrutable, diplomatic poise.

Philip IV ensured his scribes were seated behind him at a small table and began the usual courtly courtesies: introductions and anxious enquiries about the health of his 'dear cousin, Edward of England.' Corbett looked sideways at Lancaster who found this all too much, nearly choking on his fury but the French king sitting rigid in his chair, his eyes staring at a point above the English envoys' heads, continued in a dry monotone.

Philip IV, not even bothering to pause so Lancaster could answer, starkly presented the Gascon's situation as he saw it: he was overlord of the duchy, Edward may be king of England but, as Duke of Gascony, he was the French king's feudal subject: Edward's Gascon lords had attacked French property, the feudal bond was broken by Edward, therefore the duchy was forfeit to his overlord the French king. At this Lancaster could contain his anger no further.

'Your Grace,' he rudely interrupted. 'You may have good cause to seize the duchy but, by what right do you hold it?'

'Oh, that is quite simple,' de Craon silkily interjected, 'French troops are all over the duchy, so,' he spread his hands in an expansive gesture, 'we wait with bated breath for your reply.'

The English envoys had already discussed the strategies and tactics they should employ when they met the French and Lancaster, overcoming his dislike of Corbett, had asked him to intervene when he thought fit. Corbett now believed it was opportune.

'Your Grace,' he replied quickly before Lancaster made further rash remarks, 'does that mean that our two countries are at war? In which case,' he extended his hand in mimicry of de Craon, 'our meeting is over and we beg to withdraw.'

'Monsieur Corbett,' the French king's face flickered in a smile, 'you have it wrong, de Craon was only describing the situation as it is, rather than what it should be.' The English eagerly seized on the phrase 'should be' and a long protracted discussion took place on future negotiations. Corbett sat, detached and objective, aware that both de Craon and his master, Philip IV, were quietly studying him. The phrases 'allodial', 'fief', 'feudal rights and suzerainty' were bantered like feathers round the room and Corbett believed the French intended to hold on to the duchy for as long as possible. Yet, both he and Lancaster, who communicated with him in hushed whispers, also came to the conclusion that the French were not just playing for time, their seizure of Gascony being only part of a greater game.

The arguments swept back and forth across the table until both sides agreed to continue the debate at some future date. However, there were other points to raise and Lancaster came rudely to the point.

'Your Grace,' he said brusquely, 'The English agent in Paris, Simon Fauvel, has disappeared.'

'Not disappeared,' de Craon sardonically observed. 'Monsieur Fauvel, I regret to say, is dead. He was killed, probably by one of the beggar bands who roam the streets.' His words shocked the English into angry murmurs of protest.

'This is unacceptable!' Lancaster retorted. 'We are attacked outside Paris, the English king's agent is murdered in the city! Is the French king's writ so worthless that the sanctity of protected envoys can be so easily violated?'

'Monsieur Lancaster!' Philip exclaimed, 'Look at the facts, our envoys have been attacked in England: the assault outside Paris was most regrettable and you have our apologies and our assurances that the City Provost is searching high and low for the culprits. As for Monsieur Fauvel,' he added crisply, 'it would appear that your agent ignored our advice. He was out alone, at night, and contrary to our ordinances, walking the streets after curfew. Of course we regret these incidents, but there are only two, are there not?' Lancaster saw the trap and neatly avoided it. Philip was baiting them, hoping they would make some reference to the attack on the *Saint Christopher* and the death of Nicholas Poer. Corbett knew that if Lancaster raised these issues, he would have to explain the secret work both the *Saint Christopher* and Poer were involved in. Philip IV, however, was unwilling to leave the matter.

'Your master, our sweet cousin,' he commented, 'is going through unsettled times. In his letters to me he makes veiled references to treason and traitors around him.' Philip spread his hands slowly. 'But what can we do?' The English envoys, Corbett included, were too surprised to answer such an insult, so Lancaster rose, bowed and beckoned at his colleagues to withdraw.

FIVE

The meeting afterwards was brief but sombre, Lancaster neatly summarising the English position: Philip would hold onto Gascony as long as possible and only hand it back on terms fully advantageous to the French. Philip IV also believed he had the upper hand (the rest bitterly agreed with this) and intended to develop a great design or plan against Edward. The most worrying item, however, was Philip's open baiting with his insinuations that he knew there was a traitor at the heart of Edward's council, Fauvel's death and the attack on the Beauvais road only rubbing salt into an open wound. Lancaster's colleagues reacted predictably; Richmond flustered, Eastry coolly observed they had done all they could and should leave while Waterton remained silent, seemingly anxious to be away. At last Lancaster dismissed them but asked Corbett to stay. The Earl closed the chamber door and came swiftly to the point.

'I do not like you, Corbett,' he observed, 'you are secretive, too withdrawn. You have no experience of diplomacy yet my august brother has sent you here and evidently trusts you, more,' Lancaster bitterly added, 'more than he does me!' Corbett just stared back so the Earl continued, 'I suggest you were sent, Master Clerk, to search out this traitor, and may I suggest, you should begin.'

'If I did,' Corbett replied sarcastically. 'Where would you suggest I start?'

'Well,' the Earl tartly observed. 'You could continue to watch us as I, Master Corbett, will continue to watch you!'

'And secondly?'

'Discover who killed Poer and Fauvel!' Corbett would have liked the Earl to inform him how he was supposed to achieve this but the Earl turned his back, a sign that the interview was over.

So now, Corbett, accompanied by an ever-garrulous Ranulf, paced the streets, alleys and runnels of Paris. They had been given some information regarding Poer and Fauvel. About the former it was very sparse: a brief description of the man, the tavern he usually frequented and, after a series of searching, endless questioning and strange glances at his foreign accent, Corbett had finally discovered the tavern Poer had last been seen in. Not that the discovery led to much, the squat, ugly inkeeper had morosely described a man matching Poer's description who had drank and ate there on that particular evening: no, he was alone: no, he left by himself, no one followed him and the only person who had left around the same time was a crippled beggar. Corbett had tried to press the matter further but the fellow just scowled, turned away and spat.

Corbett had then decided to visit the lodgings of the dead Fauvel. He and Ranulf shouldered their way through the crowds who lined the Seine, waiting for the barges bringing produce in from the outlying farms. They crossed one of the great stone bridges spanning the Seine and walked along the alleys which twisted and turned behind the carved stonework of Notre Dame

Cathedral. Ranulf pestered Corbett with questions only to lapse into a sullen silence when his master just refused to answer. Eventually, they found the rue Nesle, a narrow alley with a deep swill-edged sewer running down its middle. The houses of black timber and dirty white plaster crowded together and rose three or four storeys high, each storey leaning over the one below. The windows were wooden shutters with the occasional one of horn and, more rarely, painted glass. Corbett found the building he was looking for and knocked on the stained door. There was a clattering inside, the door swung open and an arrogant, middle-aged woman dressed in an overblown fustian pouted at the English clerk.

'Qu'est ce que?'

'Je suis Anglais,' Corbett replied. 'Je cherche...' 'I speak English,' the woman interrupted. 'I am Devon born, my late husband was a wine merchant from Bordeaux. When he died, I turned part of this house into lodgings for English visitors to Paris. I know,' she continued breathlessly, 'you must be here about Master Fauvel, am I right?'

Corbett smiled. 'Of course, Madame, I would appreciate some information about his death.' He thought the woman might invite them in but she leaned against the door and shrugged.

'There's little I can tell you,' she replied and pointed to the muddy street. 'He was found there, stabbed in the throat!'

'Nothing else?'

'No,' she said and stared first at Corbett and then at Ranulf who was leering at her. The woman blushed at his frank, admiring smile and looked lost for words.

'There was nothing,' she stammered, 'except the coins.'

'What coins?'

The woman pointed down at the dirt. 'There, a few *sous*, nothing much, just lying in the dirt.'

'They had fallen out of his purse?'

'No, out of his hand, almost as if he was going to give them to someone.'

'Whom?'

'I don't know,' came the tart reply, 'perhaps some beggar?'

'Ah,' Corbett let out a long sigh. It was possible, he thought, just possible. He may not know why Fauvel and Poer died or who gave the order but he guessed how and by whom. Corbett turned away muttering his thanks when the woman called out.

'Monsieur, if you need lodgings?' Corbett smiled and shook his head. He would not return to this house but, judging by the look on Ranulf's face, his servant surely would.

Corbett returned to the English envoys certain in his knowledge of what had happened to Poer and Fauvel though this was only a surmise, a calculated guess and, even if it was correct, there was little he could do with the information except wait, so he decided to turn his attention to his companions. Lancaster and Richmond he tended to leave alone, Eastry was a cold fish and spent most of the time in his own small chamber, so he concentrated on Waterton. The latter had proved himself a brilliant clerk, the document he drew up summarising the meeting with Philip reflected an ordered, logical mind. As a courtesy, the English and French had exchanged memoranda of the meeting at the Louvre and Philip IV had been so impressed by the English scribe's work as to send him a purse of money as a gift.

Nonetheless, Waterton puzzled Corbett: he was secretive and withdrawn, using every opportunity to leave his colleagues to wander out in the streets and, unless his services as a scribe were needed, he would not return until the early hours the following morning. Corbett did not regard this as too suspicious for Paris and its fleshpots were an enduring attraction but, as the days passed, Waterton became even more secretive. Corbett also noticed that when French officials or messengers visited the lodgings, they always made a point of asking if Monsieur Waterton was in attendance, sometimes they brought gifts and, on one occasion Corbett thought he saw one of the French slip Waterton a piece of parchment.

Corbett finally asked Ranulf to follow Waterton on one of his nightly expeditions but his servant returned to announce he had been unsuccessful. 'I followed him for a while,' Ranulf wearily commented, 'but then a group of drunkards surrounded me and, when they found out I was English, they began to taunt and jostle me. By the time I was free of them, Waterton was gone.' Corbett his suspicions now aroused, decided to question Waterton.

He chose his moment carefully: one Sunday after Mass he found Waterton alone in his small, windowless chamber. The English scribe was seated at a table busily drafting a letter, surrounded by rolls of parchment, pumice stones, pens and inkhorns. Corbett, apologising for the intrusion, began a desultory conversation about the weather, the recent meeting with the French and the possible date of their return to England. Waterton was polite but cautious, his long narrow face showing nothing except signs of fatigue and tension. As he talked, Corbett noted his companion's very costly dress, the soft leather boots, the pure woollen cloak, hose and doublet with a frothy cambric lace showing at the neck. He wore a silver link chain round his neck and an amethyst ring on the little finger of his left hand. Quite the lady's man, Corbett thought.

'You find me interesting, Master Corbett?' Waterton suddenly asked.

'You are a very skilful clerk,' Corbett replied. 'Yet, so secretive. I know little about you.'

'Why should you?'

Corbett shrugged, 'We are all locked up here together,' he replied. 'We face a common danger, yet you wander around Paris, even after the curfew. It is unsafe.' Waterton picked up a slender, wicked-looking paper knife and began to cut a piece of vellum, drawing carefully along the ruled line and rubbing the parchment with the grey pumice stone until its surface glowed like soft silk. He stopped and looked up.

'What are you implying, Corbett?'

'Nothing. I am implying nothing, I just asked you a question.'

Waterton pursed his lips in annoyance and threw down the pumice stone. 'Look, Corbett,' he snapped. 'My business is my own. You scrutinise me like some village gossip. My father was a well-to-do merchant, hence my relative wealth. My mother was French so I am both fluent in the language and not afraid of walking about a French city. Satisfied?'

Corbett nodded. 'I am sorry,' he replied, not feeling the least contrite. 'I was only asking.'

Waterton scowled at him and returned to scraping the parchment, so Corbett left, bitterly regretting the meeting had achieved nothing except alerting Waterton and putting him on his guard.

Corbett did not share his suspicions with Lancaster who had studiously avoided him since their last meeting, moreover, the Earl had announced a date for their return to England and was busy organising the preparations. The Earl had not forgotten the attack on the Beauvais road and demanded safe conducts and an increased military escort to the coast. Philip, of course, demurred saying Lancaster did not seem to trust him so the Earl was drawn into further complex negotiations, his temper not improved by the sly innuendos and subtle taunting of the French court.

Corbett waited. The French envoys and officials visited the house and, on one such occasion, Corbett definitely saw Waterton receive a piece of parchment. He felt tempted to challenge his colleague on the spot but realised he would look a complete fool if it proved to be nothing. That same evening, however, Corbett wrapped in a heavy soldier's cloak, sword and dagger fastened to his waist, followed Waterton from their lodgings. He pursued him through a veritable maze of streets and alleyways, crossing squares past darkened houses. Corbett moved slowly ensuring he kept his quarry barely in view in case there were others, silent protectors of this night-wandering English clerk.

At last Waterton entered a tavern, Corbett stayed outside, watching the lighted doorway and square shuttered windows. The streets were deserted, except for the occasional drunken beggar or the crashing and clink of chainmail as foot soldiers, the night watch of that quarter, did their rounds. Corbett, hidden in the shadows, watched them pass in a pool of light thrown by the flickering cresset torch carried by their leader. Apart from the faint singing and clatter from the tavern, the silence was oppressive: a faint chilling rain began to fall, Corbett jumped as a rat rising among the rubbish in a corner, squealed and thrashed about as a large cat caught it silently in its killing jaws and hurried off.

The houses on the other side of the street rose, a huge dark mass above him, the night sky was clouding over, the full spring moon suddenly covered by dark rain clouds. Corbett shivered and huddled deeper into his cloak. He concentrated on the sliver of light marking the tavern door, wondering when Waterton would leave. Was he there for a night's roistering? Or was the person he was meeting already with him? Corbett cursed his stupidity, he should have at least tried to resolve that problem when Waterton first entered the tavern, now he dare not approach the door.

Corbett's anxieties were suddenly resolved by the clatter of boots on the cobbled streets. Two hooded figures stepped out of the darkness, the first entered the tavern but the second stopped in the pool of light by the door, pulled back his cowl and looked quickly around. Corbett stiffened with excitement, it was de Craon. The English clerk waited until the two had entered and, after a short while, walked across the street and peered through a crack in the shutter.

The place was ill-lit by oil cressets fixed in the wall. Corbett looked across the dirty room and saw Waterton joined by de Craon and his companion who pulled back her hood to reveal raven black hair and a face which Helen of Troy would have envied; alabaster skin, full red lips and large dark eyes. Despite the poor light, Waterton looked relaxed and pleased to see his visitors, he clasped the girl by the wrists and turning, called in a loud voice for the host to bring wine, the best he had. Corbett had seen enough and turned to go, almost screaming in fright at the dishevelled figure crouching behind him.

'A sou,' the beggar whined, 'For God's sake, a sou!'

Corbett stared at the dirty face and glittering eyes and edged away, he turned and ran like the wind down the dirty, dark street. He paused to listen for any pursuit and, though breathless, ran sobbing on, sometimes losing his way as he pounded up filthy alleys and muck-strewn runnels, slipping and gasping as he ploughed through heaps of dirt or missed his footing and splashed into the shit-strewn sewer which ran down the centre. Once he hid from the watch, on another occasion sent a poor beggar woman sprawling when she came out of the shadows pleading for charity. Corbett drew his dagger and, carrying it before him, ran on till, breathless and shaken, he reached his lodgings.

SIX

The next morning Corbett kept to his own chamber, pushing Ranulf out on some spurious errand. He was exhaused after the terrors of the previous evening. The thought of the silent horrors of those desolate streets and how close he had courted death made him feel nauseous. He dreaded the prospect of a possible return and stayed in his room for the rest of the day trying to make some sense of the chaotic information he had acquired. Waterton was half-French: he was a clerk of the royal council of England and therefore privy to King Edward's secret designs: Waterton acted suspiciously, he was courted by the French, met de Craon at night, cloaked all dealings in secrecy and seemed to have a limitless fund of money. But was he the traitor? Who was the girl? And how did Waterton pass on information to de Craon once he was back in England?

Dusk fell and Corbett got off his pallet bed. He had thought of asking Lancaster for help but he was too suspicious to confide in anyone yet he did make one request of the comptroller of Lancaster's household for certain items. The man looked startled but allowed Corbett to draw the supplies he needed. The clerk made his way down the narrow winding staircase to the hall, a low, black-beamed room with bare, whitewashed walls, a table with benches down each side, a few sconce lights and rusty charcoal braziers. The French, as Lancaster had mused loudly, had hardly bothered to make them welcome. The rooms were filthy and there was a constant wail from the buttery or the kitchen as the cooks discovered some fresh problem.

The evening meal was always a morose affair. Lancaster sat glowering at his food; Richmond, depending on his mood, was either silent or boastfully tedious as he recounted details from the Gascon campaign of 1295 which he had so badly led and so constantly justified. Eastry, after he had said the 'Benedictus', picked at his food, usually rancid beneath its sauce and spices, and kept his own counsel. Waterton ate quickly and made his excuses to leave as soon as courtesy allowed. Tonight was no different, Waterton nodded at Corbett, made the usual obeisance to Lancaster and left.

Corbett followed soon after, taking the same route as the previous evening. He soon caught sight of Waterton's purposeful walk, there was no difficulty for his quarry visited the same tavern, so the clerk hid in the shadows and began his vigil. This time Corbett not only kept the tavern door under scrutiny but occasionally stared around the gathering dusk, but there was nothing to see or hear. Only the light and faint sounds of the tavern broke the silent menace of the shadowed street.

De Craon and his companion eventually arrived, sweeping into the tavern without pausing or a backward glance. Corbett waited for a few seconds and walked quietly across the street and peered through the chink in the shutters. Waterton, de Craon and the lady sat huddled round the same table. Corbett watched but he was tense, his ears straining for any sound, his heart pounding. He wanted to run, flee from the danger he sensed was lurking in the shadows. A faint sound made

Corbett turn. The beggar was there on all fours resting on wooden slats looking up at him. 'A sou, sir, just a sou.' Corbett dug into his purse and slowly handed a coin over. Later, Corbett could not truly describe what happened even though the scene became part of his nightmares. The beggar lifted his hand and suddenly lunged at Corbett's chest, showing the dagger he had concealed in his rags. Corbett moved sideways, even as the dagger dented the hauberk he wore beneath his cloak. Corbett struck back, the dagger he carried catching the beggar full in his exposed throat and, eyes wide at the blood spouting onto his chest, the man toppled over into the mud.

Corbett leaned against the tavern wall, trying to control his terrified sobbing and stared around but there was no further danger. He looked down at his would-be assassin and gingerly turned him over with his foot. He ignored the glazed eyes, the jagged slash in the throat and searched the man but there was nothing. Corbett rose and peered through the shutters but Waterton was still close with his visitors, oblivious to the grim, silent tragedy enacted outside.

The following morning Corbett ensured Waterton had returned to their lodgings before seeking an interview with Lancaster. He told the Earl of his suspicions and what had happened the previous evening, Lancaster scratched his still unshaven chin and peered at Corbett.

'How did you expect danger from a beggar?'

'Because someone like him,' Corbett replied, 'killed Poer and Fauvel.'

'How do you know that?'

'Well, the only peson mentioned by the innkeeper near Poer was a beggar.'

'And Fauvel?'

'He was stabbed outside his lodgings. His purse was

taken to make it look like a robbery but his hand still held a few coins. I asked myself why a man should die outside his own house with coins in his hands. The only acceptable explanation was that he was about to distribute alms, a fistful of sous. Any man would be vulnerable to an assassin disguised as a beggar asking for alms.'

'But why didn't the beggar kill you the first evening?'

'I don't know,' Corbett replied. 'Perhaps I did not give him the opportunity. I fled.' The Earl slumped into a chair and toyed with the gold tassle of his gown.

'And do you think Waterton's the traitor?' he asked.

'Perhaps, but meeting de Craon is not treason, we have no proof, not yet.'

'If we trap him then it must not be in France,' Lancaster replied. 'There will be fresh opportunities.' He looked up and smiled, 'We start for England the day after tomorrow.'

Corbett was pleased to be leaving France. It was too dangerous to stay. He had killed de Craon's professional assassin and the Frenchman would neither forgive nor forget that. As for Waterton, Corbett was half-convinced he was the traitor, responsible for the death of at least two men in Paris and the wholesale destruction of an English ship and its crew. In England Corbett would gather further evidence and send Waterton to the scaffold at the Elms.

On his part, Waterton continued to act as if everything was normal, though he accepted the friendly farewells of the French officials and a further purse of gold from Philip IV. Corbett had no further chance to keep him under scrutiny for he and Ranulf spent the next few days packing their belongings and assisting with the preparations for leaving. Lancaster drove them harshly, his abrupt declaration of departure meant to take the French off their guard and so prevent any planned treachery. Horses and ponies were saddled, trunks, cases and caskets, packed at the dead of night, were hurried down and slung across their backs. Lancaster ensured some documents were sealed in pouches and others burnt. All the arms were distributed, helmets, swords, sallets, daggers and crossbows. Corbett kept the mail shirt he had drawn from the armoury and, after a meeting with Lancaster, obtained the Earl's permission to ride in the centre of the column.

The English embassy left Paris on the appointed day with banners and pennants unfurled, soldiers on the outside, clerks and officials in the centre. Outside Paris, just a mile north of the gallows of Montfauçon, a French escort consisting of six knights and forty mounted men-at-arms with a scattering of mercenaries, joined them. Lancaster reluctantly accepted their offer of protection but, overriding the objections of the knights, insisted on allocating the French to their positions. Corbett watched the stooped, lank-haired Earl and privately concluded that, though he did not fully know who the traitor was, he felt Lancaster was not the man.

As it was, the Earl's precautions proved unnecessary, the English envoys had a bruising, hasty but uneventful journey back to the French coast. Corbett was tired, harassed and saddlesore when he reached Calais though relieved to be on the verge of leaving France. Waterton was just as secretive and withdrawn as ever but did nothing to provoke further suspicion. Ranulf was positively morose, Corbett thought it was just his servant's inherent laziness yet Ranulf had more subtle reasons; he had returned to the rue Nesle and the dead Fauvel's lodgings to pay court to that haughty lady and fully enjoyed the consequences.

Madame Areras, as the lady of the house called herself, had been difficult at first, but Ranulf plied her with trifling gifts, sweet words and longing stares. Madame Areras was cold and distant as any lady in the *chansons* of the troubadours but, slowly, like a flower with its face to the sun, she opened and responded to the forceful young Englishman's wooing. Oh, there had been sighs and pretty pleas even as Ranulf removed her skirts so she stood naked before him in her own chamber. Ranulf had ignored these, patting her bottom, stroking her thighs, breasts and neck until soon they were bouncing and rolling on Madame Areras' great bolster-filled bed: the lady gasping, crying out and groaning with pleasure. Now, Ranulf would never be able to continue the affair and he glared at his taciturn master who was responsible for ending his pleasures.

Corbett ignored his surly servant and concentrated on assisting Lancaster who had laid his plans so carefully. An English cog with an escorting man-of-war was waiting in the port of Calais. Under the Earl's hard stare and biting tongue, the English stumbled aboard, men followed by horses, ponies and baggage. Lancaster did not even bother to say farewell to the French escort but stood before them, spat in the dust at their horses' hooves and, turning, stalked up the gangplank. That same evening, the English ships slipped their moorings and stood out into the Channel, heading for England.

* * *

David Talbot, yeoman farmer, squire and heir to certain prosperous lands in Hereford and along the Welsh March, was riding for his life. He dug his spurs deeper into the soft, hot flanks of his horse which leaned forward, head outstretched, its magnificent legs and iron-shod hooves pounding the shale of the rutted track into a fine, white dust. Talbot turned in his saddle and looked quickly back over his shoulder, there would be, must be, pursuit.

Morgan's men were tracking him along these narrow, twisting Welsh valleys for Talbot was a young man who knew too much. King Edward of England had promised him a fortune in gold if he brought information about a rebel leader in Wales who was secretly negotiating with the French. Well, Talbot now had such information as well as the name of the English traitor on Edward's council. He had already sent some details to Edward but this he would bring personally and so receive his merited rewards, if only he escaped the pursuit, if only he had not been found in Morgan's outhouse, examining the way the English spy had sent information to the traitorous Welsh lord.

Talbot had to escape, break out from these treacherous valleys, the hills rising out on either side of him dotted with gorse bushes which might harbour one of Morgan's bowmen. The Welsh knew these valley roads and Talbot had seen the beacons spraying into flame, sending warnings ahead. Talbot turned, his heart lurching when he saw his pursuers, black cloaks fluttering, had also entered the valley in hot pursuit. Talbot leaned across his horse's neck, urging it on with words as well as with scarring, blood-tinged spurs. The narrow valley opening was in sight, Talbot gave a cry of relief and raised himself in the saddle and this made his death instantaneous. The thin, sharp wires strung across the valley mouth sliced through his neck and sent the blood-spurting head bouncing like a ball amongst the loose shale.

SEVEN

Corbett waited outside the chamber at the far end of one of the whitewashed corridors which ran off from the great hall of Westminster. Not for the first time he turned and looked up at the timbered ceiling or wandered across to push open a wooden shutter and stare out at the royal garden beginning to bloom under a warm spring sun. Corbett had landed at Dover two weeks ago and travelled back to London, only to succumb to a fever which made his limbs and head ache. Lancaster had told him to rest in his own house while he and the others reported back to the King.

Corbett had spent days being cared for by an overzealous Ranulf, who was always anxious when his master was ill, for, if he died, he would lose his livelihood. A doctor had been summoned, who wanted to bleed him so, as he put it, the fever would be drained and the evil humours quelled. When Corbett threatened to cut his throat, the doctor quickly changed his remedies, placing a jade stone on the English clerk's stomach while feeding him a herbal concoction of wild parsley, fennel, ginger and cinnamon, all pounded to pulp and served in piping hot wine. Corbett slept and sweated, his dreams disturbed by fevers and nightmares in which he relived the horror of slaying the beggar assassin in Paris.

At last he woke, weak but cool, the fever gone. The physcian returned, genuinely amazed that his remedies had worked, the fellow gabbled instructions at Ranulf, pocketed his sizeable fee and promptly left just in case his patient took a sudden turn for the worse. Corbett soon regained his strength and, a few days later, received a royal writ ordering his presence at Westminster. Corbett wondered how long he would have to wait for by the sounds coming from the chamber Edward was working himself into one of his royal rages. At last the door was flung open and the King himself gestured at Corbett to enter. Inside, a nervous clerk was seated at a table trying to conceal his anxiety by carefully studying what he had written while Lancaster lounged in a chair, slightly forward so as to favour his misshapen shoulder.

Both the King and his brother were dressed simply in dark gowns, surcoats and mantles; jewelled brooches, clasps and heavy studded rings their only concession to fashion. The room itself looked more like a tent or a military camp; two dirty stained tapestries hung slightly askew on the wall, an iron sconce was twisted downwards and the none-too-clean rushes had been kicked into heaps. By Lancaster's look of forced patience and the mottled spots high on the King's cheeks, Corbett guessed there had been a fierce altercation between the royal brothers.

The King dismissed the scribe, glared at Corbett and waved him to a bench alongside the wall. 'Sit, sit, Master Corbett,' he snarled. 'I don't suppose you have better news for me. The journey to France was a farce, Philip outmanoeuvred, insulted and ignored you. You learnt nothing and you acquired nothing except insults. God knows, you left like whipped curs, your tails tucked beneath your legs!'

'Your Grace,' Corbett replied slowly, 'What did you

expect? Excuse my bluntness but I doubt if we will catch the spy in France. He is here in your council.' Edward glowered at Corbett, but the clerk pressed on.

'First,' he continued, ticking the points off on his finger, 'We did kill the murderer of Fauvel and probably Poer: secondly, we do know that Waterton is under suspicion,' Corbett nodded to Lancaster, 'I gave the Earl a full report during our voyage back. Finally, we do know that Philip has some grand design and the seizure of Gascony is only a part of it.' The King sat down wearily on a stool, head in his hands.

'I am sorry,' he muttered looking up. 'You, Corbett, and my brother, Lancaster, are the only ones I trust.' He tossed a greasy parchment at Corbett. 'A report from David Talbot, squire and royal retainer. It was the last letter he sent. Five days ago his headless body was found at the bottom of a Welsh valley, another casualty inflicted by Philip.' Corbett slowly read the letter from Talbot, written in a forced, clumsy style.

'David Talbot, squire, to his Grace, Edward, King of England, health and greetings. Know you that I have been most busy in your affairs in Wales in the county of Glamorgan. Know you that I have kept the castle and retainers of the Lord Morgan under close scrutiny and that the same Lord Morgan, despite being recently received into the King's peace, conspires with the King's enemies abroad. I have seen French ships off the coast and members of their crews rowed ashore and taken to the Lord Morgan's castle. I have carried out my own searches and found that the Lord Morgan has also received messengers from dissatisfied lords in Scotland. I believe, your Grace, that Lord Morgan is still hostile to your interests and is allied to your enemies both at home and abroad. The moving force behind all this is, as you know, Philip of France: he intends to destroy your Grace's patrimony in France and raise Scotland, Wales and Ireland against you. Know you that I have seen the same French ships land arms and that the Lord Morgan has new

found wealth. I beg, your Grace, to intervene here otherwise all your interests will be lost. God save you. Written at Neath, March 1296.'

Corbett looked at Edward. 'Who is this Morgan?'

'A Welsh lord, recently at war with the Earl of Gloucester, he surrendered and was accepted into my peace.' Corbett looked at Edward's strained face. 'Then why not arrest him, he is a traitor?'

'Hearsay,' Edward testily replied. 'No real evidence except Talbot's letters. Talbot himself is now dead.' Lancaster rose and shuffled to the open window.

'Look,' the Earl said quietly, 'All these are symptoms. Poer, Fauvel, Talbot and French involvement in Wales are only symptoms of a deeper disease, treachery. Find the traitor, root him out and all the rest dies.' There was silence as Edward stared at his brother.

'Waterton,' the King said abruptly. 'Waterton must be the spy, the traitor, his mother was French, he has more wealth than he should have even if his father was a rich merchant. There is more, Waterton's father was a supporter of de Montfort.'

Corbett straightened up and looked sharply at the King. In 1265 de Montfort, the great rebel against Henry III, the King's father, had finally been destroyed at the Battle of Evesham and a savage civil war was brought to a close. London and its merchants had been fervent supporters of de Montfort. Hundreds of them died or had been fined for their support. Old wounds still rankled deeply. Corbett knew that only too well, years earlier Edward had used him to seek out and destroy supporters of the dead de Montfort.

'Your Grace,' Corbett urged, 'we have enough evidence now, arrest Waterton and stop his treason.'

'Nicely said,' Edward replied, 'But evidence – do you need it?'

'No.'

'But what if you are wrong? What happens if Waterton is only a pawn? After all, he was a member of Richmond's household, it was the Earl who recommended him to my service and it was the Earl who lost my army in Gascony.'

'Do you suspect the Earl of Richmond?' Corbett asked.

'He is French, he has land there and God knows how he lost my army?'

Edward rose and paced the room. 'The French,' the King continued, 'launched their attack on Gascony in 1293. In the autumn of 1294, Brittany landed my army at La Reole and garrisoned it. In the spring of 1295, the French laid siege to the town and, within a fortnight, a fortnight! Brittany had surrendered both town and army.'

'Your Grace thinks that Brittany may be the traitor?' Corbett asked.

'Possible, it is possible.' Edward replied.

'If the traitor is here in Westminster,' Lancaster broke in, 'how do they communicate with the French? Philip has no envoys in London, all ports and ships are searched. None of our spies in the French ports have noted any exchange of letters.'

'Through Wales or Scotland?' Corbett asked hopefully.

'No,' the King replied, 'The information is sent too quickly. Philip seems to know what I have decided within days. No,' the King concluded, 'The information is sent from here.'

'Are there any letters sent to France?' Corbett asked.

'Official letters to Philip,' Edward replied, 'as well as letters to the hostages.'

'Hostages?'

'Yes, when Brittany surrendered, several of the knights could only ransom themselves by giving hostages to the French, in most cases, children. The knights write regularly to these.'

'Do any of the knights serve on the council or know any of its business?'

'No,' the King replied. 'Only Tuberville, Thomas de Tuberville. A baron from Gloucestershire. He serves as a knight of the chamber, he is Captain of the Guard.'

'Could he listen in?'

'No,' Edward answered, 'No one can listen through oaken doors and thick stone walls. Moreover, Tuberville hates the French, his letters attest to that.'

'How does your Grace know?'

'Like the rest, copies of his letters are kept in the Chancery files.'

'Talk,' Lancaster abruptly interrupted, 'All talk, everything points to Richmond. We would do well to put him, Waterton, Tuberville, anyone who has anything to do with him into prison.'

Edward rose and paced the room. 'No,' he said, 'Not yet.' He pointed at Corbett, 'You will pursue what we know. You will first visit Lord Morgan in Wales and ask him some pertinent questions.' Corbett's heart sank but one look at the cold, tired eyes of the King warned him that any objections would be ruthlessly dealt with.

A day later Corbett and Ranulf were preparing for the journey. Ranulf objected but Corbett sternly told him to carry out his orders for clothes, weapons, provisions and horses would be needed. Corbett himself wandered out into the streets, wanting to think, to reflect on his recent interview with the King. He strolled up into Cheapside, the broad highway sweeping from east to west was the main business area of the city with the Cornmarket, butchers' shambles, the Tun Prison and the Great Conduit which gave the city its water.

The boards of the traders were lowered, their protective awnings pulled out against the strong sun.

Trade was brisk in everything from a pair of hose or cherries fresh off the branch, to a pair of gilt spurs or a satin shirt with cambric lace. A funeral cortège passed, led by a friar, a quiet, sinister figure in his dark robes, pinched features staring from the cowl over his head. The mourners stumbled by, followed by the coffin on the shoulders of the bearers. Corbett heard the sobbing of the women and the deep-throated howl of a dog. Such sights seemed out of place on such a day, the crowds were out, the lawyers in fur capes on their way to the courts at Westminster: peasants in brown and green smocks coaxed their carts up to the market places ignoring the taunts and attempts at pilfer by a horde of ragged-arsed urchins. A column of mounted archers clattered by, prisoners in the middle, their hands tied to the saddle, ankles secured by chains under the horses' bellies.

A courtesan, her face painted and her brows finely plucked, stepped daintily through the street, one red, velvet-gloved hand raising her laced dress to escape the mud. She glanced coyly at Corbett and walked on. The noise and bustle was intense: tradesmen plucked his sleeve and dinned his ears with shouts and offers of custom. Corbett, regretting his decision to walk, pushed his way through the crowd into the coolness of the 'Hooded Kestrel' tavern.

It was a dirty, low-timbered room with a scattering of tables, up-turned barrels and a row of huge vats and kegs. Corbett ordered ale and a bowl of fish soup, he always found eating by himself an aid to logical analysis. He was troubled by what he had learnt: despite his victories in Scotland, the King was highly anxious, casting about like an imprisoned dog, lashing out at shadows, grasping the air and thinking it was substance. Corbett understood such anxiety but knew the traitor would only be caught through careful questioning, analysis and the application of logic. Corbett sipped thoughtfully from his tankard as he itemised what he knew about the traitor:

Item: The person was close to Edward:

Item: He had a swift, ingenious way of communication with the French which deflected all the efforts of Edward's searchers and spies:

Item: The person seemed to be a member of the Earl of Richmond's household, the same baron who had so disastrously attempted to defend Gascony just a few months ago, when, so the King implied, the trickle of vital information to the French began:

Item: It was only logical that Corbett start questioning members of Richmond's household who also had something to do with the council.

Corbett smiled to himself. He felt better and, deciding on what he should do next, left the tavern and walked back to his lodgings in Thames Street. Ranulf was surprised to see his master smile for the first time in weeks and so took advantage of the situation to ask permission to go on an errand. Corbett, smiling absent-mindedly, nodded and Ranulf was off before the clerk could change his mind, the 'errand' was the attempted seduction of some lady and there was always the chance that Corbett might suspect something amiss. Ranulf clattered down the stairs, behind him the plaintive sound of the flute his master always insisted on playing when trying to solve some intricate problem.

EIGHT

The following day Corbett was back at Westminster Palace. He would have liked to have interviewed the Earl of Richmond but 'My Lord,' so a haughty squire informed him, 'was gone on secret business of the King's.' Corbett walked off in search of Tuberville but the knight was absent on duties in the city so Corbett was left to kick his heels around the palace. He walked over to the abbey church, enjoying the warm sunshine as he watched the masons scampering like ants along the scaffolding against the north side of the abbey. Corbett was always fascinated by these magicians in stone and spent some time admiring the trellissed carved masonry, the huge grinning gargoyles depicting men, dogs, griffons and an array of grotesque faces. The abbey bells rang for prayer and Corbett wandered back to the Great Hall.

The place was thronged with lawyers, officials, petitioners and plaintiffs. There were sheriffs in from the counties to present their accounts for the Easter audit: royal stewards from the Duchy of Cornwall, their finery ruined by mud and dirt, they looked tired and harassed as they asked for directions in a strange, nasal accent. Corbett looked around, noted how many rings were left on one of the day candles and, leaving the Hall, made his way along empty stonewashed corridors to the council room.

He found Tuberville in his chamber. A man of about thirty to thirty-five summers. Tuberville seemed the typical fighting man with his close-cropped blond hair and lean, narrow features. He would have looked a predator, a professional killer if it had not been for his full mouth and anxious guarded eyes. He was dressed in chain-mail covered by a long, white surcoat bearing the royal arms of England gathered by a stout leather belt which carried a sword and dagger sheath. When Corbett arrived, he was lounging by a window, the shutters flung open for the place was a small and dusty guardroom, a table and two benches alongside the wall being its only furnishings, the floor was bare stone and the walls were covered in flaking plaster.

Tuberville turned as Corbett came in and bluntly answered his query; 'Sir Thomas Tuberville?'

'The same.'

'My name is Hugh Corbett, chief clerk to the Chancery. I am on the King's special business.'

'What special business?'

'Investigating the recent débâcle in Gascony.' Corbett watched the knight's eyes narrow in anger.

'Do you have a warrant, licence to do this?' he asked.

'No,' Corbett replied. 'Why, do you want one? I can, we can, go to the King and see him.'

Tuberville smiled, his face becoming almost boyish.

'Here,' he waved Corbett to one of the stools and crossed to a rather battered up-turned barrel bearing a tray of pewter cups and a flagon. He filled two with wine and crossed to rejoin Corbett. 'Look,' he said. 'I am sorry I was abrupt.'

Corbett took the wine. 'It was nothing,' he replied, 'Perhaps a sign of the times?' Tuberville shrugged, sat and sipped from the cup.

'Your questions, Master Corbett?'

'You were with the Earl of Brittany in last year's expedition to Gascony?'

'Yes,' Tuberville replied, 'We sailed, a fleet of ships from Southampton and landed at Bordeaux. Richmond assembled the column of march and we advanced inland to occupy the castle and town of La Reole. You may remember,' Tuberville continued bitterly, 'the damned French had already occupied a number of border fortresses and their troops were moving inland. Richmond just sat and waited: he did not try to draw the French into battle but stayed in the town.' Tuberville shrugged. 'It was inevitable. The French found the countryside deserted and their troops poured across the duchy.' Tuberville paused, staring into the cup. 'Richmond did not move, but froze like a frightened rabbit. The French encircled the town with ditches and traps to block the roads. War machines were brought up, I remember one huge bastard the French nicknamed "Le Loup du Guerre", "The Warwolf". These pounded the town with fire balls and huge rocks. We could not break out, the King was unable to send any relief so Richmond decided to surrender.'

'Was there no attempt at a sortie?' Corbett asked.

Tuberville pursed his lips. 'Yes,' he smiled 'I disobeyed orders. During the negotiations between Richmond and the French, I led a sortie, a phalanx of about sixty men-at-arms and mounted archers.'

'What happened?'

'We were driven back, the French were furious and so was Richmond. The Earl threatened me with a traitor's death for violating negotiations. I pointed out that the negotiations themselves were traitorous so Richmond ordered me to be put under arrest.' Tuberville got up and refilled his cup. Corbett watching him closely.

'What happened during the surrender?' he asked.

Tuberville stared at the wine he was swilling round his cup.

'The French, God damn them, insisted that we leave La Reole, and we did, our banners and pennants trailing in the mud, the French lined the roads and let us go with the mockery of horn, pipe and drumbeat.'

Corbett shifted in his seat. 'But you came back to a great honour, captain of the King's guard and responsible for protecting the King and his council?'

'Ah!' Tuberville smiled. 'When we returned to England, Edward read the results of the campaign and, ignoring Richmond's protests, gave me this post.'

Tuberville turned and looked through the narrow arrow-slit window. 'I must be going, I have to check the guard and ensure no threat exists to our sovereign lord.' Corbett caught the gentle sarcasm of the remark and smiled back. He liked the man, the typical professional soldier, hard, sardonic but strangely vulnerable.

'Oh,' Corbett asked, 'before you go, what terms did the French demand when they let you evacuate La Reole?'

'Hostages!' Corbett looked at the white fury in the knight's face.

'Hostages?' Tuberville nodded.

'Yes,' he explained, 'Richmond, myself and other officers had to agree to send to Paris members of our family as guarantors that, while the present troubles last, we will not fight in Gascony against the French King.'

'Whom did you send?'

'My two sons.' The reply was short, bitter and Corbett saw the hatred flare like a flame in Tuberville's eyes.

'And Richmond?'

'Oh, he sent his daughter.'

'You write to your sons?'

'Yes, letters are sent in Chancery pouches. Richmond

does the same, a copy is kept in the Muniment Chamber.'

'Do you like Richmond?' Tuberville glared at Corbett. 'If I had my way,' he replied, 'I would have had that incompetent lord, court-martialled as a traitor.' He rose, touched Corbett on the shoulder and stalked from the room.

The clerk sighed and rose to follow, he would dearly love to question Richmond but the Earl was a cousin to the King, and, if things went wrong? Corbett chewed his lip and decided it would have to wait. Nevertheless he was deeply suspicious of Richmond, something nagging at him like an old wound and he would not be satisfied till he had resolved it. He remembered Tuberville's reference to letters and decided one way to check on Richmond would be to read the copies of any he sent to his daughter.

Corbett wandered about the palace buildings and stepped into a courtyard: the royal stables took up most of the space with out-buildings, forges, piles of manure and huge bins containing oats, barley and straw. Horses, great war destriers, sumpter ponies, mules and the occasional dray horse milled in the open space before being led back to or taken from the stables. Grooms, ostlers and smiths shouted and cursed to be heard over the din of the anvil and the raucous neighing of the horses. Corbett warily crossed, keeping a sharp eye on the plunging hooves of a backing horse. He entered a small side door and went down a cold, whitewashed passage way until he reached the back of the palace and a row of chambers which housed the royal records.

Corbett knocked on the iron-studded door and was admitted by an arrogant-looking clerk. 'What do you want?'

'I am Hugh Corbett, senior clerk in the Chancery.'

'Burnell's protégé?'

'If you say so, and who are you?'

'Goronody Ap Rees, chief clerk of the records.' Corbett groaned to himself. There was, he thought, nothing so officious or trying as these pompous clerks who wielded their power like petty tyrants. 'Nigel Couville?' Corbett asked hopefully.

'I am here,' a deep grating voice answered and Couville shuffled out behind the pompous clerk.

'Why, Corbett,' the old man's lined face crinkled into a welcoming smile, his thin, cold, vein-streaked hands clasped Corbett by the shoulders. 'You should come more often,' he said softly. 'It is good for an old man to see his former students.' He turned so Ap Rees could hear him. 'Especially one of my most brilliant. Come!' He led Corbett into the small room, brushing past the furious Ap Rees.

Inside, the small chamber was packed with chests, coffers and great leather bags while shelves stretching from the stone floor to the black-timbered ceiling were full of neatly rolled scrolls, each tagged to show the month and regnal year of issue. In the centre of the room was a great oak table with benches down each side. Corbett recognised and loved the smell of red wax, ageing vellum, pumice stone and dried ink.

'What is it you want?' Ap Rees almost squeaked with annoyance.

'Certain letters,' Corbett replied, 'despatched by the Earl of Richmond to his daughter, a hostage to the court of Philip le Bel in Paris.'

'You have no right!' Ap Rees snapped back.

'I have every right,' Corbett wearily replied. He turned to Nigel Couville. 'Tell this pompous fool,' he continued, 'that if I do not have the letters written by Richmond and others to relatives held as hostage at the French court, I shall return with His Grace, the King, to continue this conversation.'

'Master Ap Rees' Nigel replied, 'is from Glamorgan, he is always telling me that things are done differntly there.' Corbett turned and looked at the narrow, pinched face of the Welshman.

'So you know the Lord Morgan?'

'I know him,' Ap Rees replied caustically, 'But I am the King's man. I have proved that in my years of service to the crown.'

'Then prove it now, Master Ap Rees, the letters please!' Ap Rees looked askance at Corbett and was about to refuse but thought better of it, shrugged and walked over to a large, leather chancery bag. He unloosed the gold-fringed, red cord, spilled the contents out onto the table and searched amongst the different scrolls and scraps of parchment. Finally, he picked one up, examined its tag, grunted and beckoned to Corbett. 'Here it is, you cannot take it away, but stay and read it here.' Corbett winked at Couville and, taking the scroll, sat at the great oak table to study it.

The manuscript consisted of small sheets of vellum stitched together, all transcribed in mauve ink by the same clerkly hand. Corbett could guess how it was done: each individual would write, or have written, his own letter before submitting it to the Chancery who would examine them to ensure they gave away no information prejudicial to the crown. The royal clerk would then transcribe the letters, making a fair copy before despatching the letters to France, sealed in a red, Spanish leather Chancery pouch while the copies were stitiched together with twine and stored away.

Corbett quickly scanned the sheets and felt a wave of compassion sweep through him; the letters invariably short, were filled with sorrow and tears as parents wrote to children, brother to brother, cousin to cousin. One of the longest was from Tuberville to his two sons. His anguish and hatred of the French were apparent, the letter, dated January, the Feast of Saint Hilary, 1295, regretted they had not spent Christmas together but he had bought them Saint Christopher medals, a wolf-hound named Nicholas and, when they returned, he would hold a great feast in some local tavern. Corbett searched on until he found Richmond's letter, a stark contrast to Tuberville's, the Earl's relationship with his daughter was cold: the Earl was formal, distinct and, most interestingly, kept referring darkly to some 'secret matter'.

Corbett, satisfied, rolled the parchment up and handed it back to Ap Rees. 'Thank you,' he smiled at Couville and nodded. 'We'll meet again, take care.' The old man beamed a toothless smile, Corbett touched him gently on the cheek and walked out into the passageway. Corbett would have exchanged a month's fees to discover Richmond's 'dark secret' and was now determined to question the Earl, not caring whether he was a rather arrogant relation of the King.

When Corbett returned to Thames Street it was dark, lantern horns had been lit and hung outside certain houses, revellers, half drunk on cheap ale and their own pleasure, burst from a tavern shouting loudly in the street. Corbett felt the hilt of the dagger stuck in his belt and gently eased his way past them. They hurled abuse but he was through and, with a sigh of relief, reached his own house and climbed the dark, twisting staircase. A decidedly dejected Ranulf was already lighting rush-lights and long white beeswax candles. Corbett asked him how things were, but only received mumbled sentences in reply. Corbett quietly smiled, Ranulf's mood meant the evening meal of wine and cold meats would be a deadly silent one.

Corbett did not mind for once the table was cleared, he left Ranulf to his own devices while he took his writing tray from a large casket and began to jot down on a scrap of parchment his conclusions and suspicions.

Item: There was a traitor on Edward's council who gave secrets to the French and communicated with the King's enemies in Wales.

Item: Waterton, the clerk, was half-French, his father had been a supporter of Earl Simon de Montfort, an inveterate opponent of Edward. Despite de Montfort's cruel death some thirty years ago, his memory was still revered in many quarters, especially in London.

Item: Waterton seemed wealthy, he acted suspiciously in Paris, being favoured by Philip as well as secretly meeting the French King's spy-master, Amaury de Craon.

Item: Waterton had been recommended to the King by the Earl of Richmond, his former patron and employer. Richmond had disastrously lost the war in Gascony, he, too, was half-French and a member of the council.

Corbett reviewed the list and sighed. It was all very well, he thought, but important questions remained unanswered:

Item: Who was the traitor? Was it more than one person?

Item: How did the traitor communicate his informaton to the French?

Corbet studied his scrap of parchment while the candles burnt low. At last he threw it to one side, logic could not help when there was insufficient information, he snuffed the candles and lay down on his trestle bed.

There was something else but it eluded him until, almost on the verge of sleep, Corbett suddenly remembered that the file of letters he had seen earlier in the day were written in a familiar hand: Corbett recalled his meeting with Waterton in the writing chamber in Paris and realised Waterton was the clerk responsible for transcribing the letters to the hostages.

NINE

The following day, Corbett sent a surly Ranulf to make enquiries around Westminster. It was almost dark when his servant returned, his temper greatly improved. 'The Earl of Richmond,' he boldly announced, 'was in the Midlands, he had been a member of a diplomatic mission to meet certain Scottish envoys for secret negotiations and would be back in Westminster by tomorrow evening.' Corbett, satisfied, spent the next two days on his own affairs: he needed certain clothes: an indenture was drawn up with the goldsmith who banked his monies and he took Ranulf to a bear-baiting in Southwark but left, sickened at the sight, and moved on to watch a miracle play, 'The Creation', staged on a huge raised platform, fashioned out of long planks thrown across a dozen carts.

Corbett felt bored by the story but admired the strange devices; the massive inflated pigskins filled with water for the great deluge, the ark moving across the stage, the flaps of metal waved to create thunder and the voice of God. Corbett stood and marvelled though he kept one hand on his purse and half an eye on the pickpockets and cutpurses who gathered like locusts on occasions such as these. The crowd was packed, students, clerks in russet gowns, the beaver hats of the merchants, the gauze veils of the ladies, the ermine-trimmed cloaks of the courtiers and gallants.

Corbett moved along, not too concerned that Ranulf had disappeared, he bought a hot pie from a baker and walked slowly through the crowd, enjoying its warmth and colour while the meaty spicy juices filled his mouth. He visited a few shops, stopped to hear a pedlar sell his wares which, to the surprise of his incredulous audience, contained the asp which bit Cleopatra of Egypt, Moses' foreskin, a strand of Samson's hair and a glossy rack which bore the image of the Archangel. Corbett always revelled in such foolery, the direct opposite of his own cold and logical life.

Darkness had fallen by the time he reached his lodgings and slowly made his way upstairs. He paused at the door, astonished by the cries and shrieks from within. He gently pushed the door ajar, stared in through the crack and saw Ranulf, naked as the day he was born, cavorting with a young girl whose red hair covered her like a veil as she twisted and turned, her white body wrapped around Ranulf, her face filled with pleasure which closed her eyes and formed her mouth into an 'O' of constant pleasure.

Corbett withdrew, angry at himself as well as Ranulf. He quietly tiptoed downstairs and went out into the street and the warmth of a nearby tavern. He chose a table near the great pine log fire and tried to dismiss what he had just seen. He felt guilty, angry and strangely envious; he was frightened of women, he had loved two and both had gone. One taken by the fever, the other, the lovely Alice, a traitor to the King. He dug his face deeper into the tankard, hoping no one else would see the tears which scalded his eyes. God knew he missed both and mourned the gap they had left. Corbett, he thought, the cold, calculating clerk, like some device from a stage, efficient, capable but lacking in warmth.

He eventually returned to his lodgings slightly drunk on ale and self-pity. He looked suspiciously at Ranulf but was too embarrassed to mention what he had seen, instead he instructed his sleepy-eyed servant to take a message to the Earl of Richmond at Westminster, to await the Earl's pleasure and bring back any reply.

The following evening Corbett, at work in his small office at Westminster Palace, was disturbed by his servant who brought a verbal reply from Richmond. 'The Earl,' Ranulf announced with malicious glee, 'was usually too busy to talk to clerks, but on this occasion he would make an exception. He would meet Corbett in the Great Hall of Wesminster just before the courts broke up. He stipulated an exact time and asked Corbett not to be late "as pressing affairs of the state" still awaited him.' Corbett immediately dismissed the still, smirking Ranulf, tidied his desk and wearily made his way along to the Great Hall. Beneath the great oaken ceiling, its timbers draped with the blue-gold standards of England, the different courts of Exchequer, King's Bench and Common Pleas, were still busy: serjeants, plaintiffs, ermine-caped lawyers, soldiers, peasants and merchants thronged in the questionable pursuit of justice. Along the tapestry-draped walls were small alcoves for lawyers and clerks to meet and Corbett went straight to the one chosen by Richmond.

He was disconcerted to find the Earl waiting for him pacing up and down, his gorgeous fur-trimmed robe wrapped about him, fastened at the neck by a cluster of pearls, set in a golden brooch. Corbett had never liked Richmond with his blond hair, watery blue eyes, red-tipped nose and mouth turned down like a landed fish. In France, he had avoided him for the Earl seemed an arrogant, waspish man full of his own honour and neglectful of everybody else's. The interview did not improve matters: Richmond described his Gascon campaign as the result of a series of unfortunate incidents. 'There was nothing I could do,' he snapped peevishly. 'The French were all over Gascony. If I had marched out to meet them I would be defeated so I stayed in La Reole, hoping his Grace would send the necessary help. He did not. So I surrendered.'

'There was no chance of withstanding a prolonged siege?'

'None whatsoever.'

'Why?'

'I had a town full of citizens, men, women and children. I could scarcely feed my own men, never mind them.'

'You objected to Tuberville's sortie?'

'Of course, the man was a fool, he was captured by the French and was lucky not to be executed by them.'

'Why should they?'

'Because he attacked them during a sworn truce. He broke the rules of war.'

'Is that why the French demanded both his sons?'

'Exactly,' Richmond stopped pacing and studied Corbett. 'Why do you ask that?'

'Oh,' Corbett replied, 'Nothing really, just that they took Tuberville's sons but only your daughter. Why?'

'None of your business.'

'Do you miss your daughter?'

'Don't be impudent, Corbett!' Richmond snarled, 'His Grace the King will know of your insubordination.'

'Then I apologise,' Corbett coolly replied, 'But one last question. Waterton, the royal clerk, he was in your household?'

Corbett almost stepped back in fear at the look of real anger which suffused the Earl's narrow, sallow face. 'Do not,' the Earl muttered softly, 'even mention that name in my presence. Now, Master Corbett, we are finished, so go! Wait!' the Earl scrabbled beneath his cloak and pulled out a small scroll. 'The King's warrant,' he sardonically commented, 'You are off to Wales, Master Corbett. I informed His Grace of your insolent request for an interview. He handed me this which is the reason I agreed to meet you. You are to travel to Glamorgan, Master Corbett. The King wishes you to pry amongst the affairs of the Lord Morgan.'

Corbett avoided the Earl's malicious smile and took the warrant. The Earl strode off in a flurry of cloak and cape while Corbett, sitting on a wooden window seat, unfolded the commission. He studied it closely but it only confirmed his worst fears: he was to bear the King's greetings to Lord Morgan but secretly gather as much information as possible about the situation in South Wales.

Corbett groaned. Wales! He had been there ten years earlier, as a member of Edward's armies as they fought their way up the narrow river valleys, cutting Wales into sections, bringing each portion under English rule. A cruel bitter war and now Corbett dreaded his return there, mixing with Welsh lords, openly obedient but secretly seething at having to accept Edward's writ, fierce fighters with their wicked daggers and long yew bows unleashing silent death along misty valleys.

Corbett rose, sighed and made his way home, his only consolation being the shouts of outraged horror when Ranulf was informed about where he was going. As matters turned out, Ranulf became strangely acquiescent and Corbett wondered if his servant had his own personal reasons for leaving the capital. He did not probe but ordered Ranulf to hire horses and sumpter ponies from the royal stables: bags and panniers were packed and, four days after receiving the warrant, Corbett and his servant were riding north-west through Acton, Gloucester and across the Severn into Wales.

Corbett and Ranulf followed the old Roman road

west as it cut through the shires. It was a soft, late spring, the vast, brown open fields being put under harrow and plough. Oxen trudged, great yokes across their shoulders, the deep, sharp plough knife cutting the ground for the sowers who followed. Above them whirled flocks of angry crows, cawing steadily at being driven from this feast by young boys who pelted them with sling stones. Villagers were coming to life after a savage winter and a cold, hard spring, so the roads were busy with carts, pedlars, huge dray horses with hogged manes and covered in black-greened leather straps.

Corbett and Ranulf stopped at taverns, houses with an ale-stick pushed under the eaves or the more welcoming luxury of the occasional priory or monastery guest house. About mid-May, the day after Pentecost, they crossed the Severn ford at Bristol and entered Wales. The clerk described to Ranulf during his journey how he had fought there ten years previously, depicting the savage beauty of the land with its dense forests, narrow valleys and wild independent tribes. Edward I had hammered the Welsh into submission, turning their petty principalities into English shires. Their great leader, Llewellyn, had been driven into the black fastness of Snowdonia and later killed; his brother, David, goaded into rebellion, had been captured, sent to London and sentenced to the abhorrent death of a traitor, hanged, drawn and quartered. Edward had then brought the Welsh to heel by appointing English officials and building huge, concentric ringed castles at strategic places in the country.

There was little sign of this forced occupation as Corbett and Ranulf made their way south, following the line of the Severn before turning inland. The countryside was noisy with sound and colour, rivers sparkled like silver as they rushed over dark crags and along winding river banks. The gorse and wild flowers were coming into colour and opening under the warming sun, so the green, mossy valley sides looked as if they were covered in costly drapes. Curlews, hawks, crows and buzzards whirled, flashes of black and white in the sky, their jubilant cawing a sharp contrast to the cool, liquid song of the thrush. The sun was warm and, at midday, both riders always stopped to rest in the cool shade of yew, oak or ash.

Ranulf acted slightly frightened, longing for the busy, narrow, noisy streets of London but Corbett loved the peace, the golden dappled colours of the woods and fields, the warm sun on his back. Sometimes, he would slump slit-eyed in the saddle feeling the cool breeze on his face and neck, listening to the bird song and the clatter of crickets and he would go back across the years to the downs of Sussex. If he concentrated, he could hear his wife, Mary, singing and the constant chatter of his baby girl. Paradise, Eden, the sun always seemed to shine there, the days were always warm until the fever came breaking into his private heaven, taking both Mary and his child. So quickly, he thought, like a cloud races across the sun, the shadow does not last long but, when it is gone, nothing is the same.

TEN

Corbett and Ranulf spent six days riding through the wild countryside of South Wales: sometimes they slept in the open, in a deserted byre or the occasional fortified manor house of an English lord. One of these warned them to be careful, marauders, outlaws and wolf's-heads still roamed the hills, even more dangerous, the lord advised, were the secret rites and rituals of the Welsh, some of whom still clung to a religion other than Christianity and celebrated their fire ceremonies in dark woods or in high places. Corbett took the warnings to heart but came to no danger, nothing worse than the mournful howl of a wolf or the screams of night creatures, as owl, fox, stoat and weasel plundered for food. The Welsh villages they passed through, small hamlets with wood and daub walls and thick thatched roofs, seemed friendly enough. Corbett could not understand the strange sing-song tongue of the people but the Welsh, small and dark, smiled and offered food and a strong fermented beer.

As they approached the craggy, sea-weeded coast around the castle of Neath, the countryside became more deserted. The occasional pedlar or merchant would jabber at them quickly when they mentioned Lord Morgan's name and, though he could not understand every word, Corbett gathered from their anxious looks that the Lord Morgan enjoyed a fearsome reputation. Corbett had acquired some information about him: Edward had conquered Wales twelve years earlier and, by 1284, all of Wales was subject to his writ, the same year a meeting of the Great Round Table had been held at Caernarvon where Edward's baby son had received the title 'Princeps Walliae' or Prince of Wales. The occupied country, however, had been restless, revolts breaking out like sudden forest fires. In 1294, two years earlier, a serious revolt had occurred and the discontent rapidly spread.

The uprising was supported by Lord Morgan angry at the encroachment on his land by Gilbert de Clare, Earl of Gloucester. Morgan received widespread support but Edward had acted quickly, marshalling armies near Chester, he advanced into Wales and crushed the rebels in a series of brilliant campaigns. Lord Morgan and other Welsh princes had to sue for terms to be accepted back into the King's peace; he was allowed to keep Neath Castle and his estates but, if Talbot's letter was to be believed, Morgan was once more plotting treason, only this time with Philip IV. Corbett had sketched in his mind a triangle of treason, at one apex sat Philip, at another Morgan, but who was at the third? The English traitor supplying them with royal secrets?

Yet, if Lord Morgan was a traitor, he still wielded considerable power: at the entrance to the Vale of Neath, a long, wide, green valley snaking through the hills, stood two massive scaffolds, thick ash poles driven into the ground, each bearing a huge cartwheel turned sideways. From the spokes of each wheel, and there must have been twelve in all, hung a corpse, its neck broken, head flapping sideways, the face black with protruding eyes and tongue whilst beneath the wheel a hapless man, nailed by the ears to the pole, a crude sign round his neck proclaimed he was a poacher.

Ranulf paled with fright and Corbett secretly wondered at the terrors awaiting them. They entered the Vale where green, fertile hills dotted with trees and rocks rose up on either side of them. The silence was oppressive broken only by the raucous call of crows or the mocking song of the curlew. From a crude map drawn up by a Welsh-speaking monk in Bristol Abbey, Corbett knew that Neath Castle lay at the end of the valley on craggy cliffs overlooking the sea. Corbett no sooner caught the first glimpse of its grey walls then he turned in alarm as armed horsemen broke from the trees and swept down to meet them.

Corbett saw the puffs of dust raised by the thundering hooves, the flash of sun on metal and the great green and gold banners which fluttered and snapped above the charging horsemen. Corbett grabbed the reins of the sumpter pony with one hand while the other searched for his dagger, a useless gesture for his assailants were around them. Corbett had seen less-likely ruffians sentenced to hang at the Elms in London; the horsemen, about twenty in number, were dressed in a motley collection of arms and armour, chain-mail, breastplates and greaves; some had helmets, conical or flat-topped but the rest wore the skins of animals, calf, wolf, otter and fox. The leader, a swarthy fellow with a black drooping moustache, was dressed in shoddy splendour, leather hose and boot, a frayed purple satin shirt beneath a rusting breastplate. On his head, the grinning face of a wildcat, its skin draping the rider's hair.

He pointed a sword at Corbett's chest and flicked his fingers. The clerk looked around; his assailants were well armed with mace, sword, club and shield, so he shrugged and handed over his dagger. 'Who are you?' The leader's English was almost perfect. Corbett stared, beneath the rags and shoddy armour, the man was educated.

'My name is Hugh Corbett, I am senior clerk in the

Chancery. This is my servant, Ranulf *atte* Newgate. We are here on the orders of King Edward of England to seek an audience with the Lord Morgan. Now, sir, who are you?'

The man stared at Corbett and burst into peals of laughter: he turned and chatted in Welsh to his companions. Corbett bit his lip in annoyance for he was sure the fellow was imitating him. Behind him, Ranulf had overcome his initial fright and was glaring round him. The Welshmen also found this funny, one of them leaned forward and ruffled Ranulf's hair, the whole group breaking into fresh peals of laughter when Ranulf reacted with a spate of filthy abuse.

Corbett himself did not say anything or attempt heroics: he knew these Welshmen, kind, courteous but, highly temperamental, they could turn suddenly violent and he had not forgotten the bodies swinging on the scaffold at the entrance to the Vale. The laughter subsided and the leader, taking the reins of Corbett's horse, led them on, the rest of the band grouped around them. The castle of Neath came into full view, a cold stark building perched on the crags of the cliffs, which rolled in a sheer drop to the sea-pounded rocks below.

A huge donjon or keep jutted above the crenellated curtain wall and, as Corbett approached the main gateway in a central tower on the wall, he could see figures, soldiers on the parapet and the huge five-horse tail standards of Morgan. There was more: a man swung by his neck from the walls and just above the gateway hung a square, red-rusted cage, the thick red chain from which it was suspended creaked eerily in the breeze.

Corbett stared and shuddered at the white bones piled in one corner of the cage. His escort seemed unpeturbed, they crossed over a narrow, deep ditch, their horse's hooves thundering on the wooden drawbridge.

Inside the cold, mildewed gateway, they paused while the portcullis was raised to allow entry into the huge yard circling the keep. This contained single-storeyed stone buildings erected against the keep, but the rest were wooden buildings, some standing free, others leaning against the curtain wall: smiths, outhouses, a kitchen, stables, a piggery and makeshift byres for cattle. A small village in itself, hens pecked and jabbed at the dirt, clucking at dogs and pigs which snouted and sniffed at everything.

Children played with the inflated bladder of some animal, babies naked as the day they were born, squatted in the dirt, their parents too busy with countless tasks. The general noise and hubub died as the mounted horsemen entered the bailey and dismounted: Corbett and Ranulf were carefully inspected, a wolf-hound came over to sniff but was booted away, then an old man, with watery eyes and crippled arms shuffled over to stare up at Corbett. He giggled, picked his nose and gently patted the clerk's sleeve.

'Be off, Gareth,' the leader said quietly and the fool, blowing kisses at Corbett, scampered away. 'An Englishman,' the leader said meaningfully. 'The Lord Morgan captured him in the wars and tried to question him. We call him Gareth for we lost his name when he lost his wits. The Lord Morgan is not too gentle with spies!' Corbett shrugged and offered the reins of his horse.

'Take care of this,' he replied coolly, 'and go tell the Lord Morgan, the envoys of King Edward are ready to see him.' He watched the Welshman's face go white with fury at the insult, his hand creeping towards the hilt of his short stabbing sword, but he thought better of it, looked around and burst into laughter. The tension drained from the group and the crowd turned back to its tasks, the newcomers seemingly forgotten.

Corbett and Ranulf were taken across the yard and up narrow stone steps to the second floor of the great keep and into the main hall. It was some thirty feet in height, and Corbett was astounded at its shabby opulence: in the south wall was a very large fireplace with a hood and mantel of square stone, Corbett supposed its chimney jutted through the thick wall to the outside. There were a number of round-headed arches about eight feet wide and splayed, these narrowed to form embrasures and narrow square windows which were glazed with the finest horn. The ceiling timbers were blackened rafters but huge drapes of many colours, some torn, others whole hung from them, while tapestries depicting scenes from the Old Testament in a wild variety of contrasting hues covered the whitewashed walls. At the far end of the hall, the dais bore a gleaming oak table on which were placed a gold jewel-encrusted salt cellar and fine silver candelabra which, Corbett suspected, were once the property of some English church. These bore lighted beeswax candles while pitch torches spluttered in brackets rusting on the wall. The floor was covered in clean rushes and Corbett could smell the crushed mint and heather which had been sprinkled on top.

The room was deserted except for two men playing chess at a small trestle table near the fire. They sat crouched in their carved chairs, cloaks about them, intent on the game. Above them, on the wooden perch, a peregrine falcon stirred restlessly against the jesses and bells on its claws, its sharp mischievous face scanning the room. The leader of the escort pushed Corbett gently, so the clerk strode across the room, studied the chessboard and moved a piece. Both players looked up, one a young, blond-haired, pallid-faced man with a girl's pink lips and cornflower blue eyes. The other, small and dark, brown hair tumbling to his shoulders, a strange contrast to the man's iron-black beard and moustache, his eyes were dark, the face as cruel and as sharp as the falcon. The younger man giggled for Corbett's move had jeopardised his opponent's game but the other just rose and stared bleakly at Corbett.

'Who are you?' he asked, his voice surprisingly low and soft.

'Hugh Corbett, royal clerk and envoy of Edward I.'

The man nodded and barked an order in Welsh, a servant scurried foward with a stool, the man waved Corbett to it, pouring him a cup of wine whilst grandly introducing himself as the Lord Morgan. Corbett nodded, sipped the wine, relishing the fine taste of Bordeaux while he studied Morgan. The Welshman was an impressive figure, gold rings swung from his ears, a silver-jewelled torque round his neck and bracelets and amethysts adorned his wrists and fingers. He was dressed in a deep blue robe trimmed with pure lambswool though Corbett saw the stains on it and the white cambric shirt beneath. The Welshman also studied the clerk, watching him warily as he sipped his wine.

'Did Owen look after you?' Morgan asked, nodding to where the captain of his escort still stood.

'Yes,' Corbett replied. 'Owen looked after me, he laughs a lot.'

'Why complain, we Welsh have little even to smile about!'

'You are discontent, my Lord?'

'No, Corbett!' Morgan sharply replied, 'I am not discontent, just making observations, as I have every right to do in my own hall, is this not right?' Morgan glared at his blond-haired companion.

'Yes,' the fellow almost lisped. 'You are certainly right.' He turned to Corbett. 'Let me introduce myself,' he continued. 'I am Gilbert Medar, steward of the Lord Morgan.' Corbett smiled warily in reply, Gilbert might be the Lord Morgan's steward, he thought, and a great deal more but this was certainly not the place to begin a debate on the subject. Morgan put his cup on the table and scooped the chess pieces back into a jewelled casket which he placed under the table.

'His Grace the King,' he said brusquely, 'has sent you to me. Why?' Corbett had expected this question, his brief interview with Edward before he left London had impressed on him one clear instruction: to find out all he could about the Lord Morgan's treasonable actions and see if they could throw any light on the traitor in London.

'His Grace the King,' Corbett lied slowly, 'sends his regards and good wishes. He is anxious that the good relations now established with you should continue: he wonders if you have caught the murderers of David Talbot and he assures you that he dismisses as malicious lies and slander, rumours that you have any communications with the King's enemy, Philip of France.' Inwardly, Corbett smiled with mischievous glee, Morgan's eyes shot to one side and the clerk felt the steward stiffen.

'I thank his Grace,' Morgan replied cautiously, 'for his good wishes to a loyal subject. Unfortunately, Talbot's assailants have not been found. The King knows that South Wales still abounds with lordless, lawless men. Finally,' Morgan spread his hands, 'I am glad His Grace has rejected any scandalous allegations about my loyalty to the crown. What else can I say?'

What else indeed, Corbett thought. He felt like laughing aloud at the mock-serious look on Morgan's face and the strained concern on that of his steward.

Two traitors and splendid liars. Corbett cleared his throat and was about to continue the diplomatic farce when a sound at the far end of the hall made him turn. A small door on the side of the dais was opened and a splendid figure walked down the hall. Corbett rose and almost stifled a gasp: she had long blonde hair parted in the middle which fell like a gauze veil down to her shoulders. Her skin was alive, fair-complexioned but clear like that of a precious stone: the face was almost heart-shaped, the nose small but the eyes held his, wide, blue and full of mischief.

Corbett had never seen such loveliness: he unashamedly looked her up and down, noting how the dark green gown emphasised the contours of her waist and breasts. She wore a brooch clasp at her throat, a silver filigree chain round her slender waist with jewelled-studded bracelets on each fine wrist. The girl stared back at Corbett with feigned shock, slightly lifting the hem of her dress.

'I am wearing calfskin boots,' she said loudly, 'and dark blue hose. Or have you seen enough?'

'I am sorry,' Corbett stuttered. 'Er, I did not expect to, I,' he rose to his feet.

'What did you expect?' the voice was a mocking sing-song.

'Nothing,' Corbett snapped, angry at himself. 'I expected nothing, I was surprised. I did not expect to see a woman here.'

'You mean in men's business, the art of war, of killing each other for the best possible motive and, when you take a rest, call it diplomacy, negotiations.'

'Maeve!' Morgan rose in pretended anger but Corbett could see he was secretly delighted to see him put abruptly in his place. 'This is my niece, Maeve,' he said, half-turning to Corbett, 'she has a fierce tongue.'

'No Uncle, I have not,' she replied tartly, 'Just the English seem discourteous, unused to greeting women,' and before Corbett could think of some fitting reply, she swept on by him. Corbett turned as he heard Ranulf, who was standing behind him, choke on his own giggles. Corbett glared at him, hiding his complete bewilderment at allowing a woman he had only met for a few fleeting seconds to so effectively silence him.

Corbett and Ranulf had no choice but to stay at Neath. Lord Morgan showed them to their quarters, a whitewashed chamber on the fourth floor of the keep containing two truckle beds, a battered trunk and a stained table with benches down each side. Corbett bitterly complained about the cold and lack of warmth so Morgan grudgingly had wooden shutters fitted to the arrow-slit windows and moved a rusting brazier as well as an iron candelabra into the room. Corbett and Ranulf could not decide whether they were invited envoys or prisoners, they were allowed the freedom of the castle and the surrounding countryside but their real home was the keep.

The great keep or donjon had three floors above ground level which housed storerooms, buttery and kitchens. The first floor was the Great Hall where Corbett had met Morgan and the second housed the solar, chapel and private chambers while the third had a collection of small, cold, stale chambers, a grandiose word for places about as comfortable as a prison.

Corbett and Ranulf lived here, at the top of a narrow, winding, mildewed staircase as did Owen, the captain of Morgan's guard, whom Corbett studiously ignored. He disliked the man with his straggly, curly black hair, sallow face and constant smile. He felt the man was truly evil; Corbett had met his type before, a killer, a man who loved death and carried its rotten stink with him.

The rest of Morgan's household lived in the basement, the outhouses of the bailey or in outlying villages. Corbett sensed that Morgan, a petty tyrant, had the undying loyalty of his feudal tenants and retainers.

The Welsh lord was undoubtedly rich, the Vale of Neath and the surrounding fertile fields ensured a steady revenue. Morgan also owned the fishing rights along the rocky, sea-swept coast and emphasised these by displaying a row of scaffolds, each bearing its rotting human carrion, stark and black against the blue summer sky. They served as a grim warning to poachers, thieves, wreckers and pirates.

Corbett often surveyed Morgan's domain from the top of the keep: it was a silent, majestic perch and Corbett loved to stand there feeling the sun and catching the salt-tinged sea breezes, a welcome relief from the stench of the *garde-robes* and latrines which spilled their muck into the moat. The clerk had tried to discover something about the death of David Talbot but all he drew were blank stares and polite smiles: if Corbett persisted, his listener would lapse into Welsh as if he did not understand what the Englishman was saying. The old fool Gareth always followed Corbett as soon as he appeared in the bailey, running alongside, imitating his walk to the general amusement of the crowd. Corbett usually ignored him.

On one occasion, however, he did question Gareth about Talbot and was sure he saw a flicker of intelligence, of recognition in the old man's eyes but then Gareth blinked, smiled slyly and, wrapping his dirty gown round him, took Corbett by the hand and led him into one of the outhouses, a long dark room, made of wattles and daub with only the door and a hole in the roof letting in any light. It reeked of leather, sweat and horse dung. Corbett peered round and saw that saddles, reins, halters, stirrups and other harness were slung across wooden bars which ran the length of the room. He turned and looked at Gareth's dreamy eyes.

'Talbot? What has this got to do with Talbot's death?' he asked but Gareth gave a toothless grin and shuffled out.

Ranulf was no more successful in eliciting information and soon settled down to ogling the women or losing any monies he had in endless games of dice. Ranulf declared he was being cheated but the Welsh just grinned and invited him to find out how. The only suspicious thing Corbett did discover was the huge pyre of faggots and brushwood stored on the roof of the keep. He supposed they would serve as a beacon if the castle was attacked or be used to boil oil or fire brands if it was under siege. Nevertheless, on one of his journeys along the coast, Corbett found similar beacons, barrels full of brushwood stacked on top of each other and he wondered if Morgan feared, even invited invasion. Corbett also noted that he was usually allowed the freedom of both the castle and the surrounding countryside but, a week after his arrival, for two days in succession, Owen politely but firmly insisted they stay in their quarters.

Apart from this, Morgan pretended to be the courteous host. Corbett dined on the high table: Lent was over, so it was an end to stale salted meat and dried herrings and mackerel, instead there was capon and sturgeon from Morgan's fish stews just outside the castle walls, the Welsh lord ignoring the rule which stipulated that sturgeon was a royal fish only to be served at a King's table. Morgan's kitchens also served venison spiced with cloves, mint, cinnamon and stuffed with almonds; fresh onions, leeks; fruit tarts and pies, junkets of sliced fruit and cream, all to be washed down with tankards of heady strong mead. Corbett noticed only one item out of place, jugs of fresh Bordeaux wine served by Morgan in his vanity to impress his guests. Corbett appreciated the wine for its taste as well as the way it clarified his faint suspicions about the beacons he had seen along the coast.

ELEVEN

During most days Corbett wandered around the castle, on occasions he attended the court held in the Great Hall. Morgan would sit on the great carved chair, beside him Father Thomas, the castle chaplain and secretary, crouched mouse-like on his stool, fearful of the things he would have to see and transcribe on the long roll of vellum before him. Most of the crimes were petty, land disputes or minor squabbles over possession. Now and again though, the authority of the Lord Morgan was challenged by a counterfeiter, poacher, outlaw or thief and punishment was always relentless, dread, cruel but, in its own way, upright and rigorous.

Corbett saw a poacher tried, sentenced and hustled from the hall: the poor malefactor was sent straight to the castle yard, his right arm extended over a block where the hissing slice of a sword took his hand off at the wrist. The man screamed in a half-faint as the executioners hurried him from the block to stick the amputated arm into a bowl of boiling pitch to cauterise and heal the bleeding stump. A few even less fortunate were sentenced to hang: one was hustled up to the battlements, a noose put around his neck and he was hoisted over to a dangling, choking death while others were taken in a great two-wheeled cart to the scaffold on the headland above the raging sea.

There was an atmosphere of terror about Neath yet the mood could alternate, swinging from one extreme to the other. At dinner, minstrels were invited to recite poems and epic stories while long-haired bards sang mournful dirges of past glories and dead dreams. Corbett had to sit through them with an equally disgruntled Ranulf. Neither could understand the songs or the conversation because Morgan insisted, most of the time, on speaking Welsh. The English envoys just had to sit there, knowing by the grins on Morgan's and Owen's faces that they were often the brunt of some cruel joke. Corbett observed that Maeve joined in though, when she laughed, it was false, the smile never reached her eyes and there were times when he caught her looking at him sideways, a sad haunted look in her large blue eyes.

A few days after their arrival at Neath, Maeve decided to break the tedium of Morgan's evening banquets and, while the bards prepared themselves with all the show and gestures professional minstrels could muster, she rose and came over to stand beside Corbett. 'Do you like our music, Englishman?' she asked, her eyes dancing with mischief.

'My name is Hugh,' he replied. 'And your music is definitely better than your conversation, though I suppose that is not much of a compliment.'

She pouted, 'Well, Huw,' she said, deliberately pronouncing his name in the Welsh fashion, 'Let us change this. You play chess? Perhaps you can teach me?'

Corbett looked at the solemn, beautiful face and loved her, biting his lip to stifle the cry which ached to burst out. He knew her serious face was a mask, secretly she was mocking him but he did not care, he could have sat and stared for eternity like some angel caught up in the eye of God. He heard a snigger and looked down the table at Owen's smirking face. 'Well,' Corbett sighed deeply, 'I would be honoured to teach you chess.' He rose and escorted Maeve over to a window seat.

Maeve summoned a servant who returned with a table, board, casket of chess pieces and a small, sconce-stone oil light. Corbett ignored the hum of conversation and the elaborate guffaw of laughter from the high table. He was only conscious of Maeve, sitting there opposite him, her heart-shaped face cupped in her hands, her eyes smiling as she explored Corbett's discomfort with her cool amused stare. The clerk laboriously explained the game, the different pieces and the more complicated moves, Maeve nodded, murmuring her appreciation before tentatively playing a few moves. Then, satisfied, eyes sparkling, she clapped her hands and announced she wanted a full royal game. Corbett obliged, it was getting dark, some of the guests had left, a few were gathered round the still droning harpists but more around the alcove where they sat. Corbett made a few desultory moves, pushing his pieces around with the murmured 'J adoube'. Maeve responded and Corbett suddenly broke out of his dream for Maeve was responding with clever subtle moves and suddenly Corbett was defeated. He stared down at the chessboard and up into Maeve's concerned face.

'You have won!' he exclaimed. 'You're...' his words were halted by Maeve's peal of laughter, clear but warm, the tears rolling down her cheeks, her beautiful, slender fingers half covering her face as she tried to control her laughter. Corbett stared at her and the grinning circle of faces. He smiled, shrugged to hide his surprise and, bowing to Maeve, rose and walked down the hall. The patter of sandals made him turn, Maeve was alongside him, sliding a slender arm through his.

'Come,' she teased. 'I can play chess better than any man!' She pressed close to Corbett, 'Unbend, man, I only jested. Come, let us take the night air from the Tower.'

Corbett smiled, hoping she would not realise how hard his heart pounded at her closeness. They made their way up the narrow staircase, Maeve resting on his arm, her hair like soft gauze teasing his face with its silkiness and fragrant perfume. Corbett withdrew the bolts on the parapet door and they walked on to the roof of the keep. It was dark, only a red flush in the west marked the sunset, a strong breeze whipped in from the sea while above them the stars gleamed like jewels in a dark room. They walked over to the crenellated wall, listening to the distant murmur of the waves and the sounds from the castle bailey below.

'I have always played chess,' Maeve broke the silence, 'ever since my parents died in the Welsh wars, I have lived here with my uncle. The skill of the game often lifts the boredom of endless castle days.'

'You are very good,' he replied.

Maeve, turning so her back was against the wall, gazed up into Corbett's face. In the faint light, the clerk could see her face was calm, serene, the mock-solemn look had disappeared. 'I have read several treatises including the poem "De Shakie Ludo",' Maeve replied. 'I always welcome visitors, they are a fresh challenge.'

'So you can read?'

'Latin and French.'

Corbett looked into the gathering darkness, 'And you are happy, I mean here, at Neath?'

'It is my home.'

'And the Lord Morgan?'

Maeve smiled. 'A strange man, you know he hates the English?' Corbett nodded.

Maeve looked away, 'Who wouldn't? They killed my parents, put half of Wales to the torch, killed our chieftains, built great castles like the one at Caernarvon and turned our kingdoms into English shires ruled by Edward's kinsmen!'

Corbet could only agree. He had fought in Wales and seen the cruelties and barbarism perpetrated by both sides: men crucified, children tossed down wells, women raped until they died. English prisoners skinned alive or nailed to trees. 'And do you hate us, Maeve.' he asked.

'No, only your desire to crush and conquer,' she turned and stared into the night, 'South Wales has seen many strange sights: they say the road below used to lead to Arthur's Camelot, that the ancient tribes, the Silures who ate human flesh and sacrificed to dark woodland gods, still thrive in the deep forests.' Maeve gathered her cloak about her and nodded towards the shoreline. 'Yet, it's the sea which brings the strangest sights, small, dark brown bodies brought in on the tide. The wise women say they come in from a land to the west.'

Corbett smiled and moved nearer the battlements. Soon, he knew, he would find out why she had brought him here. Corbett was a cynic. No beautiful woman, he reasoned, would want to be alone with him. There would have to be a reason, something she wanted. There always was. Corbett felt her hand pressing firmly on his elbow, he turned and saw her face lovely as the night staring up at him. She edged closer and kissed him softly on the lips, then she was gone.

Corbett was unused to such directness, maybe his wife, Mary, perhaps, Alice, his lover, a murderess ten years dead but she was subtle, complex and devious. Maeve was natural, relaxed and direct. The next day she sought him out and they continued the conversation and the kissing of the previous evening.

Corbett suspected she was there to watch and report on his actions but dismissed this as unworthy. She told him bluntly that he was solemn, pompous but still very funny for beneath it all he was a shy, frightened man who needed to smile more. In the following days, Corbett certainly did, as Maeve took him out to ride through the wild beautiful countryside which surrounded the castle.

She tried to teach him some Welsh words but gave it up, mocking him as too insensitive for such a subtle tongue. She drew him into talking about his past life: his wife, his work in the Chancery, even Alice and the great conspiracy in London which, ten years previously, Corbett had so successfully destroyed.

Corbett responded, cautiously at first, but soon he chatted like a child fascinated by this strange beautiful woman, so changeable, one minute coyly teasing him, the next lecturing him on Wales' past glories and the depredations of his English king.

She made no pretence about his visit to Neath. 'My uncle, the Lord Morgan,' she said on one occasion, 'is a rogue, a ruffian, a hard, fair man who hates King Edward and would gladly rise in rebellion if the opportunity presented itself. But,' she continued darkly, 'the price of failure is too great. He has rebelled once and has been pardoned. The next time he may suffer the same fate as the great Prince David, Llewellyn's brother.' Corbett let the matter rest. He was frightened lest Maeve provoke a quarrel by openly accusing him of being a spy. Corbett was also wary of Morgan, who might take offence at an Englishman paying court to his niece, but surprisingly, the old rogue just laughed and clapped him on the shoulders. It seemed, Corbett concluded, that Maeve was the only person the Lord Morgan was frightened of.

Owen, the captain of the garrison, was a different matter. He smiled more but his dark eyes glistened with a murderous malice whenever they met, and even

Ranulf, now immersed in the daily routine of the castle, begged his master to be more careful. Corbett heeded the advice. Once, Maeve took him down to the castle bailey where Owen was drilling his men. Hugh was used to the mounted phalanxes of English knights, a feast of colour as armoured men in chain-mail and plate armour covered in bright heraldic designs, charged and counter-charged with sword, mace and blunted lance, according to the rules of the tournament and tourney. But this was different and when Owen saw Maeve and himself on the steps leading down from the keep, he selected one of his men and staged a mock fight as much to dazzle Maeve as well as warn the Englishman.

Corbett felt jealous as Maeve clapped her hands and cried out in amazement at Owen's prowess but even he grudgingly praised the Welshman and quietly vowed that if it ever came to a fight, he would have to kill Owen with the first blow for the man was a born warrior. Owen and his opponent fought on horseback, sturdy, surefooted garrons, who wheeled and turned as their riders pressed with knee or thigh. Both men were lightly armoured in chain-mail shirts, boiled leather leggings and boots, their heads protected by conical helmets with cheek and noseguard. Each carried a small round shield and, because this was a mock fight, blunted swords which could still inflict a serious wound. The riders charged and circled each other. Owen's swordsmanship drawing the gasps of the onlookers as he whirled and dodged so it seemed horse and rider were one. Time and again, Owen ducked under his opponent's guard, smacking the flat of his sword against the unfortunate man's stomach and chest.

Finally, Owen tired of the game, broke off and cantered away, his opponent charged, sword extended, the hooves of his horse pounding the ground, Owen swerved his own horse to meet him but never seemed to reach a full gallop. Corbett mischievously thought Owen had become over confident and would be bowled over by his opponent. The riders met, Corbett saw Owen dive beneath his assailant's swinging sword and, as the man charged past, Owen checked his own horse almost bringing its haunches down into the dirt while he swung his own sword to catch his opponent on the back of the head and send him crahsing senseless to the ground. The onlookers cheered, Owen took off his helmet and, raising his sword, saluted the now breathless, pink-cheeked Maeve. Corbett he dismissed with a long murderous look.

The English clerk was not unduly worried except by Maeve's passion for, whenever they rode out, they often kissed, embracing more passionately, more demanding. Corbett wanted to make love and hoped Maeve would invite him into her chamber. Only once, did he allude to this but received the tart response that her maidenhead was not a gift to some passing Englishman. Corbett believed she was frightened of him leaving and, now in his fourth week at Neath, he knew Edward would be impatient for his return whilst his continued presence was beginning to heighten the tension in the castle. Maeve wanted him but hid her feelings behind bitter-sweet mockery. Morgan just ignored him, Owen stalked him like a hunter whilst Ranulf, bored but now fearful of Owen's open hostility, began to plead with his master about the date of their return to London.

Corbett anxiously wondered if Morgan would allow them to leave safely and, even if they did, would Owen and his men obey such an order? What really concerned Corbett, however, was King Edward's expected reaction: he had learnt very little at Neath and what he had would not be new: Morgan was ripe for rebellion but there was no evidence, nothing to connect him with the French or the traitor on Edward's council. Oh, Corbett, had questioned where and whenever he could but the blank stares continued: Maeve was the same, she remembered Talbot, even the day he left Neath Castle for good.

'There was,' she remarked, 'a fierce quarrel between Talbot and Owen, Talbot demanding to be allowed to leave as he was on the King's business, Owen reluctant to allow him.'

'Why?' Corbett asked. 'Why should Owen detain Talbot?'

'I don't know,' Maeve crossly replied, her brows coming together as they did when she was angry, 'All I heard was Owen shouting that Talbot had been amongst the saddles!'

'But that does not make sense. Saddles? What are so special about the saddles?'

'God knows,' Maeve replied. 'My uncle bawled at Owen to let Talbot go, but not before riders were sent out warning scouts that Talbot was on his way. A short while after he left, Morgan sent Owen and a troop of horses after him.' Maeve shrugged, 'Who cared for Talbot? He was an English spy. No one here mourned for him.'

Corbett felt like asking if she thought he too was an English spy and, more importantly, if anyone, particularly her, would mourn his death?

TWELVE

To John Balliol, by God's grace and with Edward of England's permission, King of Scotland, the very walls of Stirling Castle seemed to drip with sweat and glisten in the midsummer heat. Swarms of flies spawned in the putrid dung heaps in the courtyard below came in through the open window and hovered above a table littered with fragments of food and pools of spilled wine. In his thick, gold-encrusted robes Balliol felt hot, hotter than he had ever had in his whole life. His body was soaked in sweat and he noticed a trickle of dirt run from beneath a cuff of his frayed gold robe. He tried to ignore the chatter of the bishops and great ones of Scotland as he stared down the table looking in disgust at the discarded meat, soiled bread platters and huge pools of red Bordeaux wine.

The latter seemed to gleam like great globules of blood and Balliol, blond-haired, thin-faced, gazed with his rabbit-like eyes and wondered if the wine acted as a warning, a prophecy of what might come. After all he was plotting against his overlord, Edward of England, and, although Balliol was frightened of everything and everyone, Edward of England held a special terror for him. Only God knew when that terrible man would march north, the heavy dust of his great baggage trains hanging over the roads of Scotland which would be scored by the hooves of his war-horses, warning the Scots that once again Edward of England, the Hammer of their kingdom, had arrived.

The English war host was a splendid and terrible sight, a moving forest of death, but, as Balliol knew from his constant recurring nightmares, the real terror was the tall figure of Edward, encased in black armour, mounted on a gold caparisoned, black destrier, his yellow hair now white with age streaming in the wind, his tough old body held fast in a cuirass of steel. Balliol wondered if the wine prophesied that when Edward heard of Balliol's plotting, once again he would invade Scotland and his great army devastate the kingdom from the Tweed to the foothills and mountains of the north. Balliol sighed and moved his backside on the hard chair. He felt his queasy stomach grumble and churn, accompanied by a sharp stab of pain, and once again he experienced that deep depression at his own inadequacies which so affected his health that even here in the council chamber he could not control his body.

Balliol was a man who had wanted to be king but now he had achieved the crown, realised how dreadful the responsibilities were. Scotland was a sprawling mass of fighting factions; the barons of the Lowlands despising the clan chieftains of the north; the Lord of the Isles, with his sleek, low-slung galleys, ever ready to go to war against all and sundry. How was he supposed to keep the peace? Years previously the true king of Scotland, Alexander III, had fallen mysteriously to his death leaving no apparent male heir.

The Scottish lords had squabbled amongst themselves over the succession and Edward of England, like some great black cat, had sat and watched them weary each other before intervening, solemnly adjudicating that the nobleman with the best claim was Balliol. Once Balliol accepted, Edward imposed very strict terms and conditions which made the King of Scotland no more than a vassal of the King of England. Balliol, of course, had objected and, time and again, Edward had returned north to remind him of his obligations. Balliol knew that he was not strong enough to withstand Edward, never mind his own barons, and writhed with embarrassment as he remembered some of the humiliating experiences inflicted upon him; being summoned by English merchants before Edward's courts to answer like some common lackey for his actions and decisions.

Of course, the great Scottish lords, led by the Bruces and the Comyns, had watched all this with wry amusement, sniggering behind their hands, laughing at him, calling him Edward's puppet or mammet, yet Balliol had no choice but to submit humbly, seething with anger.

However, now it was different, salvation had come from an unexpected quarter. Philip of France had overrun Gascony, maliciously pointing out to Edward that he was as much France's vassal as he claimed Balliol was his. But there was more, Philip had weaved alliances in the Low Countries as well as with Eric of Norway and he wanted Scotland to be part of France's great design against Edward of England. Balliol at first refused, hesitant, fearful of what Edward might do or say, but then Philip had given him assurances that England faced trouble in South Wales as well as in Gascony and worse would come for Philip had a spy on Edward's council. A man close to Edward, who sold the French everything Edward thought, decided or planned to do. The French claimed that this traitor could be the key to unlock Edward's strength and drain it just as much as Philip Augustus, almost over a hundred years earlier, had unlocked the key to the power of Edward's grandfather, King John, and drove him out of Normandy.

Balliol had promptly summoned his council to Stirling and surprised them all by announcing his intention to overthrow Edward's rule, seek an alliance with France and Norway and compound this alliance by his own marriage with Jeanne de Valois, Philip IV's cousin. At first the barons and bishops had been horrified, then delighted to see their king for the first time in his reign act like one. There had been discussions for hours on the best method of achieving this and Balliol smugly watched them all, revelling for the first time in a true notion of kingship and power. Nevertheless, his terror of Edward still held him fast. He looked down at the bishops and barons, so eager to advise and counsel him. Wolves, he thought, savage men, who, if he failed this time, would assuredly tear him to pieces.

At last, tired of the confusion and chaos in the hall, Balliol raised his wine cup and slammed it down on the table. He banged it harder when, with annoyance, he realised that everyone ignored him, and shouted shrilly for silence and order. Slowly, his counsellors stopped their individual discussions and looked towards him.

'My Lords,' Balliol said, realising how he was almost imitating Edward's voice and manner, 'My Lords, we have decisions to make. We know that Edward is weakened by this traitor on his council and now faces formidable alliances led by our friend, Philip of France. It is our intention to renounce homage to Edward and seek an alliance with the French. Is this your wish?'

A loud chorus of 'Ayes' and roars of approval greeted his words and Balliol smiled, nodded and slouched wearily back in his chair, oblivious to the conversations which broke out further down the table. Neither he nor his counsellors noticed the young squire who slipped from the hall, made his way down to the castle yard through the great cavernous gateway and into the town.

Robert Ogilvie, squire to the Scottish court, was in fact a traitor. He had heard news and information which he knew the English emissary in Stirling would pay gold for, the identity of the traitor on Edward of England's council. That ninny of a king, Balliol, had virtually announced who it was but the rest of the council had been either too inebriated or insensitive to grasp it. Except Ogilvie, who had dreams of wealth and power, and the secret he carried would make them real.

Ogilvie made his way down the narrow, dung-strewn street which stank like a midden in the summer heat. He saw a ragged, one-armed beggar man drive off some yapping mongrel and the sight of another man's wretchedness made him hug himself with pleasure. He was young, he was able and soon he would be rich. He hurried on through the market place, ignoring the cries of the hawkers and the pedlars with their tawdry geegaws and the trash they usually sold, and entered the cool darkness of the tavern lit only by the sunlight which poured through two rough-hewn windows. In the far corner of the room his English counterpart was waiting for him.

'Well,' the Scottish clerk thought, 'not really English, more Welsh.' He had come here ostensibly on business connected with Edward of England and stayed hoping to garner whatever information he could. Ogilvie smiled as he crossed the room, he had news which would set this arrogant Welsh clerk by his ears.

Goronody Ap Rees was pleased to see Ogilvie. He had been sent by Edward of England to spy and this young cockerel of a Scot would make it worthwhile. He ordered the best wine and, after the slattern had served them, generously poured cupfuls for the Scotsman to gulp whilst only sipping his own. He listened carefully to the Scotsman's chatter, sifting the wheat from the chaff, the gossip from the truth, the facts from the scurrilous items Ogilvie seemed eager to press upon him. He sensed the squire had something important to say and realised that, given enough time and enough wine, he would. Eventually Ogilvie, flushed with wine, paused, took a deep draught from the cup and slammed it down on the table.

'I have,' he announced loudly, 'some special news, but it will cost you.' Ap Rees nodded, expecting this, and the Scotsman launched into his startling revelations. Ap Rees listened, concealing his own excitement and once Ogilvie had finished, pulled a clinking, leather purse from his pouch and threw it across the table.

'You have earned this, Scotsman!' he said, 'You have earned it well' and, without further fuss, rose and quietly swept out of the tavern. Ogilvie, much the worse for wine, stared down at the purse, carefully picked it up, hid it under his robe, gulped the remains of the wine and rose to leave.

The two men in the far corner had watched this little tableau and, after Ogilvie had staggered out, broke their watchful silence.

'Do you think Ogilvie told him?'

'Of course!' the second replied, 'That is why the purse was passed.'

'And what now?'

The other shrugged.

'Edward's emissary has his news. And Ogilvie?'

The first man turned and smiled bleakly at his companion. 'Oh, he served his purpose. Make sure that you are with him tonight and cut his throat!'

THIRTEEN

By the sixth week in Neath, Corbett was perplexed and tense like a dog left on its leash. He had discovered nothing, he did not want to leave Maeve but felt increasingly trapped as the Lord Morgan courteously ignored his requests to return to London. The days dragged by so slowly that the resolution of his difficulties took him by surprise, coming quick like a sword leaving its sheath or the hum of an arrow through the air.

On the Tuesday, just after midsummer, the castle was caught up in a frenzy of activity. In the evening Corbett and Ranulf returned to their chamber to find Owen dressed in black skins perched like some evil bird on the narrow shelf of one of the window embrasures.

'I bring messages from the Lord Morgan,' he sang out, 'You are to be detained in your rooms.'

'Until when?' Corbett snapped, 'The same thing happened a few weeks ago. The Lord Morgan has a strange idea about hospitality. Why does he treat us like this? What does he want to hide?'

Owen jumped down like a cat and stood so close that Corbett could smell his stale odour and see his slanted, amber-flecked eyes.

'Lord Morgan,' Owen replied, 'Can do what he wants in his own castle and in his own domain, remember that,

Englishman!' He brushed past Corbett and lightly skipped down the stone spiral staircase.

Owen was right. Morgan did what he liked and Corbett and Ranulf were virtual prisoners in their chambers until the following Monday. It was an experience neither would want to repeat: Corbett prowled round the room, snapping at Ranulf or lay on the small truckle bed and morosely glaring at the ceiling, wondering what Morgan was up to, even though he had a shrewd idea.

Corbett also knew that, despite his love for Maeve, he would have to leave Neath empty-handed. The King would be furious for Corbett had acquired nothing for his six weeks stay in Wales. Ranulf tried to comfort him, offering to show him how to play dice, cheat and win but got little thanks for his effort. Their meals were brought to them, Maeve visited but Ranulf's presence curtailed any enjoyment of each other's company and the encounter was limited to Corbett's questions about what was happening and Maeve's evasive answers. There was a constant guard on their chamber, four or five of Owen's cut-throats lounged in the narrow passageway outside their room and the only time they were permitted to leave was to use the *garde-robe* in a corner near their chamber.

Corbett did his best to find out the reason for their detention and spent a great deal of time asking rhetorical questions intended for no one, though Ranulf did his best to answer them. At last the young man, becoming tired of this angrily expostulated that Corbett could easily find out the reason for their temporary imprisonment. 'What do you mean?' Corbett snapped.

'Why, Gareth, the fool,' Ranulf replied, 'He wanders round watching everything.'

'But he's witless!'

'No,' Ranulf smiled. 'He only appears to be, offer him a few coins and he will soon talk sense.' Corbett grunted and rolled on his side but a grain of an idea had taken root.

Late the following Monday morning, a grinning Owen ordered the guards away and announced that Corbett and Ranulf were free to go where they wished, and that included returning to London. The same evening, Lord Morgan repeated the invitation, openly insinuating that the English had outstayed their welcome and should be off, Corbett threw an anguished glance at Maeve, who bit her lip but almost imperceptibly nodded her head. Corbett could understand what she was trying to tell him though the next morning Maeve seemed to avoid him, Morgan and Owen boldly ensuring they did not meet and talk.

Corbett also sensed a change in mood in the castle; the retainers were more distant, the servants and other hangers-on open in their disdain. There was an air of menace, of silent danger gathering in the dark recesses of the castle. Corbett, despite his training in the halls of Oxford, as well as in the legal niceties of the Chancery and the Exchequer, trusted his instincts and believed he was in danger and should either fight or flee. Nevertheless, remembering Ranulf's advice, he searched out and found Gareth squatting in the corner of the parapet walk on the curtain wall.

'You are well, Gareth?' The man smiled, saliva dripping out of his mouth. Corbett looked quickly around and, digging into his purse, drew out a silver coin.

'This is for you, Gareth, if you tell me about the ships which have just gone.'

Corbett watched Gareth intently, certain he saw a flicker of recognition, of intelligence in the watery eyes.

'What ships? What does Master Englishman want to know about the ships?'

'So you know there were ships?' Corbett crouched and pulled out another coin. Gareth glanced quickly around, his eyes sliding like bubbles on water.

'Three ships,' he whispered and stretched out his hand.

'Ah,' Corbett withdrew. 'What ships?'

'French,' Gareth replied. 'I said to myself they are French, flying their great blue and gold pennants. Oh, a brave sight, Master spy.'

Corbett stared at Gareth and smiled realising Ranulf was right, this man only acted the fool. Gareth confirmed his suspicions: the French were visiting Neath, their ships finding it easy to slip into the deserted coves along the desolate coastline of South Wales. This explained the beacons, Morgan's secretiveness as well as his wine cellar, though Corbett suspected the French brought arms and stores as well as tuns of red Bordeaux. Philip was intent on raising a rebellion in Wales and Morgan was his chief ally but was there a link with Philip's spy on Edward's council?

Corbett emptied his purse and showed Gareth a clutch of coins.

'They are yours,' he said, 'if you can tell me why Talbot died?'

Gareth wiped saliva from his slack lips and stared at Corbett, the vacuous expression in his eyes, replaced by a wary cunning. 'Master Talbot,' he drooled, 'was an inquisitive man who also paid,' he stretched out a be-grimed claw-like hand and Corbett dropped a few coins into it before drawing back.

'Gareth,' he added warningly. 'You are trying my patience.'

Gareth smiled. 'Master Talbot had a quarrel with the Lord Morgan.'

'What was said?'

'Nothing, except the Lord Morgan accused him of

prying where he should not.'

'Anything else?'

'No, except I heard Talbot, Master Talbot, that is, mention something about saddling. I suppose he intended leaving, there was something else.'

'Yes. What?'

'A man called Waterdoun.'

'You mean Waterton?'

'Yes, I think so for I heard both Lord Morgan and Master Talbot use that name.'

'Is there more?'

Gareth turned, looking slyly out of the corner of his eyes.

'Oh, no,' he replied. 'That's all Gareth knows. Truly, so why not pay Gareth his money.'

Corbett handed the rest of the money over and rose to go. He heard footsteps on the stairs leading up to the parapet walk and hastily distanced himself from Gareth but Owen came tripping up the stairs and stood, legs apart, blocking Corbett's path. Dressed in black, Owen looked like some sleek, well-groomed crow, his glittering eyes stared at Corbett and then beyond to where Gareth say huddled in terror.

'So,' the Welshman said in his half-sung tones, 'the Englishmen have been talking and now Master Corbett has to be away. Ah well,' he stood to one side and mockingly bowed with an ornate flourish of hands for Corbett to continue down the steps. The clerk turned and looked pityingly at Gareth crouched like a frightened rabbit, there was little he could do and he had to prepare himself. Clutching the dagger beneath his cloak, Corbett glared at Owen and passed him by and, throat dry, his heart thudding with fear, he walked slowly down the steps, half expecting Owen to challenge him, listening intently for the hiss of steel as sword or dagger were pulled from their sheath.

Nothing. Corbett reached the bottom and continued his journey across the castle yard and up the steps into the keep. Once inside, he closed the door and leaned against the cold, grey stones as he tried to control the terror which had drenched him in sweat and threatened to turn his bowels and legs to water. He breathed deeply, gulping the air until his heart ceased its beating and the warmth seeped back through his body.

Corbett wanted to stay hidden in the dark gloom but he knew he had to prepare himself, he sighed and made his way slowly up to his chamber, leaving the door ajar while he hurriedly packed saddle-bags, ensuring the purses, warrants and secret memoranda were carefully filed away. He searched the bottom of the largest trunk until he found what he was looking for and lifted it out, his ears straining for any sound on the steps behind him. He heard the soft scuff of a boot and turned praying it would not be Ranulf. He adjusted the saddle blanket on his arm, watching as the door pushed open and Owen slid like the figure of death into the room. He carried a sword and Corbett saw the blood splashes on its edge and tip.

'You look as if you expected me, Englishman?'

'I waited for you, Owen,' Corbett looked down at the sword, 'and how is Gareth?'

'Oh,' Owen smiled brilliantly. 'Gareth is dead. I always thought he only acted the fool. I told the Lord Morgan that many a time but, as you have found out, he has a soft heart, like Maeve his niece!'

'Like Maeve his niece,' Corbett repeated, mocking the words, glad to see the slight flush of anger in Owen's face. 'And you, Master Welshman,' he continued, 'Why are you here, Owen?'

'To kill you, Englishman!'

'Why?'

'Firstly, you are English. Secondly, you are a retainer

of the English King, and thirdly you are a spy and, finally, because I want to.'

'Why, because Maeve loves me?' Corbett taunted.

Owen anrily threw his head back snorting with laughter and Corbett waited no longer. He let the blanket drop, jerked the clasp of the small, steel-meshed crossbow and the jagged bolt was speeding for Owen's chest even as he lowered his head, catching him just beneath the heart and flinging him back against the half-open door. Owen groaned and looked in surprise at Corbett as he crumpled to the floor. A great dark stain circled the bolt embedded firmly in his chest and a light red froth seeped between his half-open lips.

'Why?' he whispered, 'like this?'

'Like all killers,' Corbett replied, 'you talk too much.'

But Owen could no longer hear, he groaned, coughed blood, his head sagging forward as he quietly died. Corbett crossed and felt Owen's neck, guilty at the warmth he still felt there but relieved there was no beat of the heart. He jerked up, clutching for his dagger as the door was pushed open shoving Owen's corpse onto its face. Maeve stood there, her face as white as snow, mouth open, her bosom heaving to suppress the scream.

'Hugh!' she exclaimed. 'I saw Owen walk across the bailey with his sword drawn, I knew he was coming, I expected...'

'To find Owen alive and me dead? Corbett interrupted.

Maeve nodded, her face still white with terror. She looked down at Owen.

'He is dead?'

Corbett nodded. 'He killed Gareth and came over to murder me.'

'Why?'

'Why not?' Corbett snapped back and slumped

wearily on the bed. 'Maeve,' he added slowly, 'you know why I was sent here. I know your uncle is conspiring against the King. He must stop. Philip of France is only using him. Owen knew I was a spy and he hated me for that as well as for loving you.'

'And do you?' Maeve picked her way over Owen's body and came to stand next to Corbett. 'Oh, Englishman,' she said, 'I stand in my own castle with the corpse of a man who would have championed me against the world, yet I neglect him because of an Englishman, a spy who says he loves me. And do you? Do you really?'

Corbett grasped her white clenched hands in his and drew her to him to kiss her. 'With all my heart,' he muttered fiercely. 'So, leave with me, Maeve. Now, come!' She kissed him gently on the forehead and stroked his cheek, tracing with one finger the furrows around his mouth.

'I cannot,' she whispered, 'but,' she drew herself together briskly, 'you must. Now! No!' She stopped any protest by placing her fingers gently against his mouth. 'You must go, my uncle will kill you for Owen's death. You must not take your horses but leave by sea. I will show you.' She stared round the chamber. 'Get Ranulf!' she ordered. 'Now!'

Corbett rose and was about to speak but saw her determined look and meekly complied.

He found Ranulf ensconced in one of the outhouses, hiding like the rest of the garrison from the fierce afternoon sun. He was wearily attempting to seduce a girl who persisted in talking in Welsh and so refused to accept or acknowledge any of his compliments. Corbett dragged him outside and whispered what had happened and, stifling the young man's exclamation of horror with a vicious rap on the ankles, returned to their chamber in the keep. Corbett was now concerned that the garrison would soon rouse itself from its slumbers, questions would be asked and he had no illusions about what would happen if they were in Neath when Owen's corpse was discovered. Maeve was still in the room.

She had filled and fastened their saddle-bags. Ranulf gave a small moan of fear when he saw Owen's corpse but Maeve told him to be quiet and beckoned for them to follow. They slipped quickly down the steps of the keep, past the main hall where Corbett was alarmed to see some of the retainers beginning to stir. He heard the yelp of the spit dog, a small, crook-backed creature fastened to an iron post and made to press the cogs and wheels which turned the massive spit. Voices shouted, a cat scuttled by, a mouse in its jaws. Maeve led them out of the keep and, following its line, rounded a corner and stopped while Maeve fumbled with the heavy clasp on a wooden, iron-studded door.

Corbett anxiously looked around; the garrison was waking from its afternoon slumber, a girl sang softly, a dog stretched and yawned, impervious to the flies buzzing in a halo about his head. Soon the silence would be broken by a scream or shout as Owen's or Gareth's body was discovered. Maeve fumbled with the catch again and Corbett tried to control his panic, shifting uneasily under the heavy saddle-bags slung across his shoulders, beside him Ranulf almost whimpered with fear. At last, the door creaked open. Maeve whispered for them to be careful as they cautiously went down a row of slippery steps. Pitch-coated torches flared and flickered in their rusty clasps, the wet, slime-ridden walls gleaming in the light.

At the bottom of the steps, Maeve pulled a torch from its holding and led them along a cavernous tunnel, picking her way daintily around puddles of slime and mud. There were other tunnels leading off the main passage and Corbett realised that these led to the dungeons and storerooms of the castle. Maeve led them on, once she turned and demanded total silence with an imperious gesture. Corbett coughed once and immediately saw that the sound echoed along the tunnels like the crash of armoured feet. He stopped, froze like a hunted rabbit but, urged on by Maeve's gestures, followed her deeper into the passageway. It became darker, colder and Corbett wondered where they were going: a stiff, cold breeze caught the flame, teasing and making it dance. A rat slithered across their path squeaking in anger and, above his head, Corbett heard the rustle and flutter of bats. A distant, clapping thunder, like the hoof beats of mailed horsemen just before they charged, made him stop until he realised it was the roar of the sea.

The cave became lighter, damper, they turned a corner and Corbett almost gasped in relief at the sunlight blazing through the cave mouth. They left the tunnel, Corbett looked around, behind him rose the sheer cliffs of Neath while across the sand and shingle, the sea thundered under a clear blue sky. Maeve stopped, paused and pointed along the coastline.

'If you keep to the line of the cliffs you will come to a small fishing village.'

She slipped a ring shaped in the form of a Celtic cross from her finger and handed it to Corbett.

'Leave this with Griffith, a fisherman. Say I gave it to you, he will take you along the coast and across to Bristol.'

'Maeve, can you, will you not come?'

'Hugh, you must go, please! This is the only way across, my uncle's men would only catch and hunt you down.'

Corbett held her hand and smiled.

'And Lord Morgan does not control the fishermen of the seas?'

'No,' Maeve replied. 'You must know such rights were granted by your King to the Earl of Richmond. My uncle is negotiating to buy these rights.'

She caught Corbett's startled gaze. 'Why, what is the matter?'

'Nothing,' he muttered. 'Nothing at all.'

'Then be gone,' she kissed him lightly on the lips and turned to go.

'Maeve,' Corbett took his dead wife's ring off his finger. 'Take this, remember me!'

She nodded, grasped the ring and slipped quietly back into the tunnel.

FOURTEEN

Corbett turned, the beach seemed more desolate, the sun had lost some of its golden brilliance. He wanted to stay, to call Maeve back and realised how much he had come to accept her presence, like a man used to a warm fire, misses the heat when he moves away. Above him, hunting gulls screeched their lonely call, Corbett felt the desolation creeping in like mist from a marsh. He rubbed the side of his face and looked back at where Ranulf was digging the sand with the toe of his boot and awoke to the real danger they were in.

'Ranulf,' he called softly. 'We must leave, the tide will come in and trap us against the cliffs.'

Groaning and cursing, Ranulf picked up the fat, heavy saddle-bags and followed. They stayed under the brow of the cliffs, hidden from the eyes of any scout or watcher. Corbett also wanted to avoid disturbing the gulls and cormorants wading in the lazy foam-edged sea: a sudden flurry of birds would only draw attention. They walked on as the summer sun began to sink, a ball of orange streaking the sea with fire. There were no signs of pursuit and Corbett hoped Morgan, probably misled by Maeve, would be scouring the Vale of Neath, sending out search-parties, sealing off the valley mouths in an attempt to trap and kill them. The only real danger was the sea, now noticeably closer as the tide crept in threatening to cut them off. Corbett urged Ranulf on ordering him hoarsely to keep close and walk faster.

They rounded a bluff and Corbett almost shouted with pleasure. The cliffs suddenly swept down into a little cove and on their edge was the small fishing village Maeve had mentioned. Corbett told Ranulf to keep under the lea of the cliffs as they made their approach, Morgan's retainers might be in the village and he did not wish to walk into a trap. Corbett left Ranulf at the foot of the track and quietly made his way up to the brow of the hill, squatting behind some fern he watched the scene before him. The village was a collection of wood and daub huts, each in its own plot protected by a flimsy fence. The thatched roofs swept down almost covering the square open windows, very few of them had doors, the square opening being protected by a thick sheet of canvas or leather. Near the huts were long slats or planks slung between poles of dead ash where the fish were gutted and dried.

A pile of refuse lay beneath and even where Corbett sat the smell of decaying fish and other odours made him feel nauseous. The village was quiet, a few children, almost naked save for a few rags, played in the dirt clay alongside rooting, fat-flanked pigs and stinking dogs. Now and again, a woman would push back a leather doorway and call out to a group of men who sat on a bench before one of the huts, drinking and playing a desultory game of dice. There was no sight of any of Morgan's men. Corbett heaved a deep sigh, stood up and walked into the village.

One of the mongrels dashed towards him, its ugly head forwad, upper lip curled in a snarl of anger, it snapped and lunged with its rat-trap jaw. Corbett lashed out with his boot and the cur turned and ran as one of the men rose, shouting and gesticulating.

Corbett walked towards him. 'Griffith,' he said, 'the lady Maeve told me to ask for help.'

The man, small, thick-set with a balding head and skin the colour and texture of leather, simply stared back, one huge muscular hand stroking the thick, jet-black beard which fell to his chest. He replied in Welsh but Corbett was certain he understood English.

'The lady Maeve sent me,' Corbett repeated, 'She told me to give this to Griffith.' He opened his hand and showed the ring which the man swiftly took.

'I will keep this,' he replied in fluent English. 'I am Griffith: what does the lady Maeve want?'

'To take me across the Severn to Bristol.'

Griffith groaned, shrugged his shoulders and turned away. He walked over to the small group of onlookers and turned.

'Come!' Griffith waved his hand.'Come!' he repeated. 'We go!'

'Now?'

'Why not?'

'The tide is turning,' Corbett protested, 'we cannot leave?'

Griffith looked at him with blue, child-like eyes.

'We may stay if you want,' he replied, 'but we have learnt that Lord Morgan's men are scouring the countryside, we can wait till they visit here if you like.'

Corbett grinned and hoisted the saddle-bags further up his shoulder.

'You are quite correct,' he replied, 'We should leave as soon as possible.' Griffith nodded, brushed past him and led Corbett down the path to where Ranulf was waiting for them. Griffith stopped, looked and beckoned him to join them.

They crossed the wet sand to where the fishing smacks were drawn up, lightly fastened to great stakes driven down into the sand. Griffith unfastened the largest, a long, low-slung craft which was already provisioned for sea, with water casks and two earthenware pots and Corbett realised that in normal times, Griffith and his fellows would wait for the evening tide, to go out and to ply their nets. Moaning and groaning, they pushed the boat to the water's edge, it was a cumbersome task till the waves caught the boat like a man catches a lover, then it became alive, bobbing and turning on the waves eager to break free of the land and make its way out to the open seas. Griffith climbed in, followed by Corbett and Ranulf: the Welshman grabbed the tiller while Corbett and Ranulf were ordered to man the oars and row. Griffith sat grinning like a devil while he ordered the two Englishmen to pull, loudly cursing every time they strained gasping over the oars.

'Come gentlemen,' he mocked, 'you must row for your lives, well away from the land where we can wait for the tide to turn.'

They did until the sun sank in flashes of red into the sea. Only then did Griffith order them to rest and, for a while, they collapsed on the benches breathless, until Griffith roused them with cups of water and slices of dry fish.

They refreshed themselves feeling the boat rise and dip under the swelling tide, Griffith loosened the huge square sail and they drowsed while the boat ploughed through the sea under a clean, clear summer night. Corbett did not care for the night, the breeze or the dark blue sky iced by a summer moon and clear stars. While Ranulf slept, he crouched in his cloak and almost wept at the deep sense of loss at leaving Maeve. He was like that for most of the eight day voyage, too depressed even to feel seasick or choke on the simple fare Griffith provided. Once or twice he tried to draw the Welshman out on the lady Maeve and, when that failed, questioned the man about the Earl of Richmond's negotitations with the Lord Morgan over fishing rights along the South Wales coast but Griffith refused to answer.

They continued on their voyage, which lasted over a week, favoured by warm winds which brought them into the sea roads into Bristol where all three, visibly relaxed to be in English waters, watched the huge cogs, men-of-war and merchantmen leave or arrive at the great port. They disembarked at evening, squeezing between two huge fat-bellied cargo ships. Corbett offered Griffith gold, the Welshman took it without a word of thanks and, dumping the saddle-bags on the cobbled quay, walked back to his boat.

Ranulf was almost beside himself with happiness to be out of Neath. Corbett felt the same relief but it only covered the pain at leaving Maeve and the frustration that such a dangerous journey had achieved so little. They picked up their bundles and made their way along the busy wharfside: past sailors from Portugal, small and swarthy with gold or pearl-encrusted ear-rings, arrogant Hanse merchants in their dark colours and expensive beaver hats. There were Flemings, Rhinelanders, Hainaulters and Genoese, their different tongues and outlandish clothes reminded Corbett about the story of the Tower of Babel in the Bible. It was warm and he felt light-headed and unsteady after days in the fishing smack drinking stale water and eating salted fish.

They left the wharves, Corbett pulling Ranulf from staring at the scaffolds, black and three-branched, each bearing the corpse of a river pirate rotting in the summer sun and sentenced to hang there for the turn of seven tides. The clerk and his servant made their way into the town, across the huge cobbled market place where traders were taking down the striped awnings, poles and trestle stalls under the watchful gaze of market officials.

A group of drunks, still singing and revelling, were led

off to sober up in the long range of stocks on a platform at the far end of the square. A pedlar, still desperate for trade, hoarsely shouted his wares; pins, needles, ribbons and geegaws. A thief was pelted with offal as he sat near a huge horse trough: dogs and cats fought like warriors over the pile of refuse, carts trundled away, wheels crashing, while their drivers, peasants with their families, slumped exhausted after a day's arduous trading.

Corbett and Ranulf stared at it all, a stark contrast to the strange, outlandish routine of Neath Castle. Ranulf looked hungrily at the taverns, Corbett, wondering what Maeve was doing, testily urged him on. They walked through the market and entered a maze of streets where the huge, half-timbered houses loomed like trees above them. Corbett had already decided where to stay and gave a cry of relief when he left the streets and took the rutted track which led up to the Augustinian monastery.

The clerk vaguely knew the Prior and trusted their acquaintanceship backed by royal letters and warrants would ensure a welcome. He was not disappointed: an ancient, ever-smiling, lay brother ushered them into an austere guest room, served them with stoups of ale and muttered that the Prior would join them as soon as Vespers ended. He then sat opposite them, smiling and nodding, as Corbett and Ranulf drank the ale.

Eventually, as the priory bells boomed out, the Prior bustled in, he embraced Corbett, clasped Ranulf's hand and speedily agreed they could stay. Two small cells were provided, their walls still gleaming from fresh coats of lime whitewash. Both men bathed, sharing a huge tub or vat in the monastery laundry room and, after changing their soaked, salt-encrusted cloaks, went down to the rectory.

Afterwards, Ranulf decided to wander in the

monastery grounds catching as he said in crude mimicry of Corbett, the best of the evening breezes and, openly ignoring Corbett's order to see to their belongings, sauntered off. Corbett glared at his retreating back, sighed and made his way down to the chapel. It was dark and cool, the dusk only just kept at bay by huge candelabra whose pure flames sent the shadows moving like ghostly dancers. At the far end of the sanctuary behind the carved chancel screen, the monks were standing in their stalls chanting Compline, their words rolling like distant thunder, echoing the pure notes of the leading cantor.

Corbett squatted in the nave at the base of a huge rounded pillar and let his mind be caught and soothed by the rhythmic singing. He heard the cantor's *'Dixi in excessu Meo, omnes homines Mendaces'* – 'I said in my excess all men are liars', Corbett ignored the deep-throated response of the monks. Were all men, he wondered, liars? Were all women? Was Maeve? He felt the bitter-sweet sense of her loss clutch his heart. Would he see her again? Would she remember him, or let the memories seep away like water in the sand? The monks intoned the paean of praise which marked the end of their office: *'Gloria Patri, Filio et Spiritu Sancto'*. He sighed, rose, stretched his cramped muscles and walked through the cloisters to his cell.

There, he took his writing case and penned a swift letter to Maeve which he hoped the Prior would give to some trader, pedlar or fisherman. Corbett sealed it with a blob of red wax, realising it would take weeks, if ever, before it reached Neath.

Then, quickly he scratched down the conclusions he had learnt:

Item – There was a traitor on Edward's council.

Item – The traitor was corresponding with the French and, possibly, traitors in Wales.

Item – This treachery had begun after the Earl of Richmond's disastrous expedition which had lost England the Duchy of Gascony.

Item – Waterton the clerk: his mother was French, his father a rebel against the King: he lived beyond his means, was courted by the French and secretly met Philip IV's spy-master. He was a former clerk in Richmond's household and also seemed to have some connection with Lord Morgan of Neath.

Item – Was Waterton the traitor? Or was it his master, the Earl of Richmond?

Corbett stared into the darkness but only saw Maeve's lovely face and felt a cold loneliness grasp his soul in its iron-hard fist.

* * *

Robert Aspale, clerk of the Exchequer, felt equally lonely. He had been sent to France by the King as his agent to oversee matters there. By 'oversee' Edward, of course, had meant 'spy'. The King had been most insistent that Aspale leave, adding that his emissary to South Wales, Hugh Corbett, had failed to return or even communicate with the English court. It should have been Corbett, Aspale thought, here, in this tavern on the outskirts of Amiens, but Edward had said he could wait no longer and so Aspale would travel to Paris posing as a merchant from Hainault. He would enter France through the territory of Edward's ally, Guy Dampierre, Count of Flanders: Aspale was fluent in the different tongues and dialects of the Low Countries and posing as a cloth merchant looking for fresh trade in the great markets of Northern France would prove easy.

Secretly, however, Aspale was to discover if any of Edward's agents and spies in Paris were still alive as well as try to unearth the secret designs of Philip IV. He carried a belt round his slim waist, its pouches filled with gold which could open doors and, more importantly, loosen tongues: courtesans, petty officials, impoverished knights, servants and retainers. They all heard gossip, bits and pieces which collected together like fragments of a mosaic, could form a clear picture of what was happening.

Aspale stared round the crowded tavern, he felt comfortable after his meal of duck cooked in a thick, spicy sauce and washed down with deep gulps of Rhenish. He suddenly noticed a petite girl with hair as red as fire tumbling down to her shoulders. She was wearing a tight green dress which emphasised her jutting breasts and slim waist before falling in a flounce about rounded ankles. She was pale, her skin looked as smooth as alabaster, only her arrogant, heavy-lidded eyes and twisted, pouting mouth marred her beauty. She gazed boldly at Aspale, nodded slightly and, after a few minutes, left the table where she was sitting and moved across to join him. Her French was fluent though Aspale detected the softer accents of Provence.

'Good evening, Monsieur,' she began. 'You have enjoyed your meal?' Aspale gazed back speculatively.

'Yes,' he replied. 'I have enjoyed my meal, but why should that concern you?' The woman shrugged.

'You look content, happy, I like to be with a happy man!'

'I suppose you search them out?'

The girl threw her head back and laughed. She smiled dazzlingly, the merriment in her eyes clearing the angry sulkiness from her face. She leaned across the table.

'My name is Nightshade,' she murmured. 'Or that is what I prefer to call myself, and you?'

'Van Greeling,' Aspale lied good-humouredly. 'And now, Lady Nightshade, a drink?'

The girl nodded and Aspale ordered a fresh jug and two clean cups.

The Englishman was under no illusion about his companion's true calling but he was tired, slightly drunk and totally flattered by this young courtesan's attention. They chatted for a while as the tavern filled and became more noisy, Nightshade refilled his cup, leaned over and whispered in his ear. Aspale saw the unflawed whiteness of face, neck and breast and caught the faint fragrant perfume of her hair. He wanted this woman and, tiring of banal conversation, quickly agreed that they should move upstairs to a private chamber. Nightshade said she had one and rose.

Aspale, half drunk, staggered to his feet and followed her through the crowd, careful lest he slipped in the dirt and refuse which littered the straw-covered floor, his eyes intent on his companion's fluid, rounded hips. They climbed the wooden staircase. Aspale followed Nightshade to a corner chamber, impatient as she fumbled at the iron clasp. The door swung open and Nightshade stepped into the pool of candelight. Drunk as he was, Aspale sensed there was something wrong. Who had lit the candle? It was too well prepared, Nightshade turned, her face drawn, the smile gone, her eyes haughty and sad. The door crashed shut behind him, Aspale scrabbled for his dagger but the assassin had the garrotte around his neck and Aspale's life flickered out like the flame of the candle.

FIFTEEN

Corbett and Ranulf took four days to reach London, the Prior loaning them the best horses from his stables, Corbett solemnly promising that the royal household would ensure their safe return. The journey back was peaceful, no danger of outlaw attack for the roads were packed with soldiers moving south to the coast as the King, having crushed the rebels in Scotland, was now determined to take an army to France.

Corbett sat and watched the soldiers march past: most were veterans, professional killers in their boots, leggings, boiled leather jackets and steel conical helmets. They were all well armed with a dagger, sword, spear and shield and marched by oblivious to the dust clouds and haze of swarming flies. Corbett let them pass, the troops showed that King Edward's patience had snapped and was now determined to settle the quarrel with Philip by force.

Corbett rode on through Acton and into the city. They reached their lodgings, checked their possessions, Ranulf taking the horses to the royal stables and promptly disappearing into the shady swirl of Southwark's low life. Corbett resignedly accepted this and spent two days regulating his own affairs before sending a message to the royal palace of Westminster that he had returned. If Corbett thought the King's absence would provide him with a respite he was swiftly disappointed. The following morning, a group of royal serjeants armed with warrants arrived to take him to Westminster where Edmund, Earl of Lancaster, was waiting in the sacristy of the abbey church.

There, among the splendid silken capes, silver candelabra, crucifixes and chalices, Corbett gave the Earl a brief summary of his visit to Neath. The Earl, dressed informally in silken shirt and hose, slumped in a great oaken chair and heard him out. Corbett, ignoring the look of anger on the Earl's pinched features, reiterated the obvious conclusion that the visit had achieved little, dismissing with a lurch of his heart, Maeve's sweet face and beautiful eyes. When he finished, Lancaster sat, head to one side, a gesture which only emphasised his crooked frame. At length he smiled wearily and rose.

'You failed, Corbett. I know,' he raised a be-ringed hand to fend off any questions, 'You did your best. When I say "failed" I mean you discovered nothing new except confirm our suspicions about the traitor.'

'You know who he is?'

Lancaster grimaced. 'It must be Waterton,' he replied. 'It has to be. These are your conclusions and we have fresh evidence.'

'Against Waterton?'

'Yes. My brother is in the north bringing Balliol to heel. The Scottish King's defiance lasted days but it did serve us well for one of his squires, Ogilvie, told our spy in Stirling that the Scots had learnt that Waterton was the spy.'

'How did they know?'

'From the French!'

'But they could have just said that to protect the real traitor!'

Lancaster shrugged. 'But why bother,' he snapped, 'in

protecting someone that does not need any protection. Anyway,' the Earl concluded, 'someone evidently thought Ogilvie had done something very wrong. A few hours after he met our spy, he was found with his throat cut.'

The Earl paused to pour himself a cup of wine. 'There's more,' he continued. 'On our return from the embassy, the chancery bags and pouches were emptied. A large fragment of Philip's secret seal was found in the pouch used by Waterton. Which means,' Lancaster testily added, 'that Waterton must have received some secret message from Philip IV.' Lancaster pursed his lips.

'Of course, it may have been a mistake, it may have even been put there but,' Lancaster sighed, 'all the evidence points to Waterton.' The Earl jabbed a finger, dismissing further questions. 'Enough,' he snapped. 'You are to visit Waterton. He has already been arrested and committed to the Tower and,' Lancaster smiled maliciously, 'after that you are, at the King's express command, to return to France with Philip's envoys and see if you can find anything new.'

Corbett groaned at the thought of France but he had no choice in the matter. He nodded his reluctant agreement to the still smirking Earl who rose, patted Corbett on the shoulder and swirled his great cloak around his body.

'The French envoys are now awaiting us,' he said, 'We had better meet them.'

The Earl swept out of the room, Corbett following him down to the great council chamber. Lancaster sat on the throne in the centre of the dais, gesturing at Corbett to join him on his right; other members of the council took their seats as, amid the shrill bray of trumpets, the French entered the chamber led by Louis of Evreux, Philip IV's brother, resplendent in a blue ermine gown, a jewel-encrusted brooch swinging against his chest, glittering rubies, pearls and diamonds sparkling on his gloved hands. Evreux carried his head proudly as if it was something precious and unique, he sat on the chair opposite Lancaster, his entourage taking up position alongside him whilst the clerks and scribes from both sides arranged themselves round a side table.

Lancaster and Evreux began the meeting with the usual diplomatic platitudes; Evreux mourning the absence of Edward and smirking when Lancaster, flushed with anger, snapped back that trouble in Scotland prevented the King being present. The process of Gascony then began, both sides repeating their long lists of grievances. Corbett let the sonorous speeches slip by like water in a steam. He had glimpsed de Craon sitting on Louis Evreux's right. The French master spy had also seen him but avoided any direct glance so Corbett glared at him. Was de Craon surprised to see him? Corbett thought so but the Frenchman's face was impassive as he carefully listened to the list of grievances presented by the English. Corbett sighed and, not for the first time that day, thought about Maeve. Her face stayed in his mind like a sanctuary lamp flickering brightly against the darkness, whilst the memory of her soft blue eyes and long blond hair haunted the innermost reaches of his soul. He wished she was here amongst these grave, self-important men whose thoughts and words would, in a year, be mere dust.

Suddenly, he heard raised voices and broke from his reverie. Louis was taunting Lancaster, achieving considerable success for the Earl was virtually shouting in reply. Corbett felt the rising tension, even the scribes looked sideways, pens poised as they helplessly wondered what would happen next. Corbett glanced at de Craon and caught the sardonic gleam of triumph in the Frenchman's eyes; God, Corbett thought, they bait us here in the very Palace of Westminster. He remembered the attack outside Paris, the vibrant loveliness of Maeve and felt a terrible rage surge through him. Corbett whispered into Lancaster's ear, urging the Earl to say something to halt the constant taunts from the French.

'My Lord of Evreux!' Lancaster called out pulling himself free from Corbett, 'I must apologise for the tumult and discord on our side but this is due to special circumstances.' He looked around, evidently pleased at the way his words silenced the clamour in the hall. 'We have,' Lancaster bluntly continued, 'just ordered the arrest of a man close to our counsels, a veritable viper in our bosom, who gave our secrets to the King's enemies here and,' he added, pausing for effect, 'across the seas.'

His words were greeted by a hum of consternation from those English standing behind the French envoys. Corbett ignored them, closely studying the reactions of the French: Evreux did not seem disconcerted whilst de Craon continued to pick at a loose thread in the sleeve of his gown before turning to whisper to Count Louis. Corbett had set the trap, he now waited for the French to step into it.

'My Earl of Lancaster,' Evreux called out, 'We are pleased that our English cousin has been freed from such an irritation. We hope this viper is not involved in the negotiations with us for, if he has betrayed you, he could well have betrayed us.'

'Is that all, my Lord?' Corbett was surprised to hear himself speak. Evreux looked at him disdainfully.

'Of course,' he replied. 'What else is there?'

'What else?' Corbett thought to himself, ignoring Lancaster's curious glances and de Craon's hostile stare. He had sprung a trap upon the French, years ago in

Scotland and now he had done it again. He was sure of it. He clenched his fists in excitement, not bothering to concentrate as the discussion reverted to more boring, desultory matters.

It was late afternoon before the process was completed and, as Lancaster later sardonically commented, there was a great deal of talking but little was said. The French believed there was a way to settle the dispute, saying it was a pity the English king was not present but, and here de Craon had looked meaningfully at Corbett, King Philip IV would personally explain to Edward's envoys his ideas for the resolution of all difficulties. The French then presented their sworn safe conducts for the English envoys who were to accompany them back to France. When Lancaster announced it was Corbett, de Craon smirked whilst Evreux looked offended as if he had expected someone of higher rank. The meeting broke up, Corbett patiently listening to Lancaster's angry exclamations before leaving for the Tower and his interview with Waterton.

A flimsy wherry boat took him up the crowded river past the docks, the steelyard, the galleys and ships pouring wealth into London and the pockets of its merchants: the light craft of the fishermen, petty traders, the scaffolds with the bodies of hanged pirates, their souls gone, fleeing through their blank eyes and yawning mouths. Around them, the living ignored this grim reminder of death in the pursuit of wealth; a spritely barge drifted by, its smart, black woodwork gilded and draped in costly cloths, pennants and banners which proclaimed its importance more loudly than a fanfare of trumpets.

The boatman guided his craft under the towering arches of London Bridge. The water roared and frothed as if in a giant cauldron, Corbett felt afraid but the boat shot through as straight and true as a well-aimed arrow. The turrets of the Tower loomed up above the trees: the great keep built by William the Norman now ringed and protected by walls, towers, gulleys and moat. A fortress to keep London quiet; the King's treasury and record office but also a place of darkness, terror and silent death. In its dungeons, the King's torturers and executioners searched for the truth or twisted it to suit their own ends.

Corbett shivered as he climbed up on to the Tower wharf; it was a calm, soft, golden evening but blighted by his mission to this place. He walked across the drawbridge and began his journey through a series of sombre gateways, places built for trapping and killing any attacker. He was stopped at every turn and corner by well-armed, hard-eyed young men who searched his person and examined scrupulously the warrants and letters he carried. One of these became his guide, a shadowy, mailed figure who led Corbett on, his head and face hidden by a steel conical helmet, he marched in front, hand on sword, his great military cloak billowing out like the wings of a giant bat. They came out of the range of walls, many still covered with scaffolding ropes, as King Edward tried to strengthen the Tower's defences and on to a large grassy area which surrounded the great, soaring Norman keep.

Here, in the innermost bailey of the Tower, lived the garrison and its dependants; two-storeyed wooden houses for important officials such as the Constable and Steward, huts for workers, as well as stone kitchens, smithies and outhouses. A few children played, hopping around the great war machines, the battering rams, mangonels and catapaults which lay round the bailey, their silent menace and threat of death drowned by the games and cries of the children. Corbett's guide crossed to the keep and, following the line of the wall, walked round its base to a small side door.

Corbett entered, a deep sense of dread closing at his heart and stomach, he knew he was entering the dungeons and torture chambers of the Tower. He strained to hear the bird song and distant shouts of the children. He wanted to clutch the sound to his chest to comfort him. The door slammed shut behind him; his guide struck tinder-flint, took the flaring sconce torch out of its socket and beckoned Corbett to follow. They went down the wet, mildewed steps, at the bottom was a huge cavern, Corbett shivered when he saw the braziers filled with spent ash, the long, blood-soaked table and the huge pincers and jagged iron bars which lay along the damp, green-slimed walls. Torches flickered throwing shadows across the pools of light, ghosts, Corbett thought, the souls of dead, tortured men. The common law of England forbade torture but, here in the kingdom of the damned, there were no rules, no common law, no regulations except the will of the Prince.

They walked across the sand-strewn floor and along one of the tunnels which ran from this antechamber of hell down under the base of the keep. The light was poorer here; only the occasional rush-lights: they passed a series of small cells, each with its iron-studded door and the small grille. They turned a corner and, almost as if he was waiting for them, a fat turnkey, dressed in a dirty leather jerkin, leggings and apron, scuttled forward like a spider from the shadows. Corbett's guide mumbled a few words, the man jerked and bobbed, his fat face creasing into an ingratiatory grin. He led them on, stopped at a cell, fumbling as he drove a large key into the lock. The door swung open, Corbett took the sconce torch from the soldier.

'Wait here,' he said, 'I will see him alone.'

The door crashed behind him and Corbett held up

the torch, the cell was small and dark, the rushes had turned to a soft oozy mess on the floor, the stench was terrible.

'Well, Corbett. Here to gloat?'

The clerk raised the torch higher and saw Waterton on a low trestle bed in the far corner. His clothes were now a collection of dirty rags and, as Corbett stepped forward, he saw the man's unshaven face was bruised, the left eye almost closed while his lips were swollen and flecked with blood.

'I would rise,' Waterton's voice was terse and clipped, 'but the guards are none too gentle and my ankles have swollen.'

'Stay,' Corbett urged. 'I have not come to gloat but merely to question, perhaps help.'

'How?'

'You have been arrested,' Corbett answered, 'because we think, or rather the evidence points to you being the traitor on Edward's council.'

'Do you think that?'

'Perhaps, but only you can disprove it.'

'Again, I ask you. How?'

Corbett stepped closer and looked at Waterton. The man was sullen, brave but, in the flickering light of the torch, Corbett saw the fear lurking in his eyes.

'You can explain your wealth?'

'My father deposited a great deal with Italian bankers, both the Frescobaldi and Bardi families can attest to this.'

'We will see. And your father?'

'An opponent of King Henry III.' Waterton bitterly commented, scratching an open sore which seemed to glare out through the shreds of his leggings.

'Do you share his views?' Corbett quietly asked.

'No. Traitors swing to a choking death. I do not want that.' Waterton eased himself up, the steel gyves chafing his wrists, the chains clanking in protest.

'And my mother,' he almost jibed, 'Is it high treason for her to be French?'

'No,' Corbett snapped, 'But it is high treason to consort with the French.'

Waterton jerked up the chains screeching and clashing as the man moved in fury.

'You cannot prove that!'

'So, you do not deny it.'

'Yes, I do,' Waterton snarled, 'Don't be such a clever bastard, stop putting words in my mouth. I do not know what you are asking.'

'In Paris,' Corbett answered, 'In Paris, the French paid special attention to you, singling you out for favours and gifts.'

Waterton shrugged wearily.

'I did not know and still do not, why such favours were shown to me.'

'Or why you should meet de Craon and a young, blond woman, secretly at night in some Parisian tavern?'

Even in the dim light of the sconce torch Corbett saw the blood drain from Waterton's gaunt face.

'I do not know what you mean!'

'By God you do!' Corbett shouted, 'Are you the traitor, the spy? Did you send Aspale and others to their deaths? An entire ship's crew? For what? To satisfy the itch in your cock!'

Waterton lunged forward like a dog, teeth bared, his usual saturnine face twisted into a snarl of rage. Corbett stared at him as, held back by the chains, the man clawed furiously at the air.

'Tell me,' Corbett continued as Waterton slumped sobbing, back on to his filthy bed. 'Tell me the truth. If you are innocent, in hours you'll be free but now you are in deep mire, held fast as any fly in a spider's web.'

Corbett paused. 'Why did the French favour you? Who was the girl you met with de Craon? Have you been in correspondence with Lord Morgan of Neath?'

Waterton breathed deeply.

'My father was a rebel against the crown,' he began slowly. 'But I am not. My mother was French but I am not. My wealth is my own. My allegiance is to Edward of England. I do not know why de Craon favoured me. I was the clerk responsible for sending the King's letters to him but I would no more correspond secretly with that treacherous Welshman than you!'

'And the young woman in Paris?'

'That, Corbett, is my affair. My only secret. For God's sake!' Waterton shouted, 'If every man who secretly met a woman was charged with being a traitor, then we are all dead men.'

'Tell me her name!'

'I will not!'

Corbett shrugged and, turning, knocked on the cell door.

'Corbett!'

Hugh turned and flinched at the hate in Waterton's eyes.

'Listen, Corbett,' he rasped, 'If I told you, you would not believe me, not you. You're a lonely man, Corbett, a righteous man with a sharp brain and a dead soul. You may have loved once but now, you have forgotten even how to. So why should I tell you? I hate you, your cold emptiness, from the very bowels of Hell, Satan and all his demons will surely come to fill it!'

Corbett turned and banged on the door. He wanted to get out, he had come to make Waterton face the truth and now hated having to confront it himself.

SIXTEEN

Six days later, after a quiet and uneventful journey, Corbett and the French envoys landed at Boulogne-su-Mer. Corbett was accompanied by an ever-grumbling Ranulf, angry at being snatched away from the pleasures and joys of London's low life. Another Englishman accompanied them, William Hervey, a small, mouse-like man, a scribe by profession and timid by nature. He was used to working in the Court of Common Pleas and was totally overawed by the company in which he now travelled. The French left them alone. De Craon and Corbett exchanged pleasantries but, in the main, the relationship, if one could call it that, was one of mutual distrust. Actually, Corbett felt safer with the French than he had since his return from Wales: they had guaranteed the safety and security of his person; awesome oaths sworn over sacred relics and the Bible that he would be allowed a safe return to the English court.

Lancaster had also given him a stream of verbal instructions; what to say, what not to say, what to offer, what not to offer, when to leave and when to stay. Corbett ignored most of them. He realised that the Earl was telling him to seek the best offer he could get and accept it. It was openly agreed at the English court that Philip, now faced with war in Flanders brought about by

English agents, could not contemplate similar action in Gascony if Edward took his army there.

Consequently, the French king would probably agree to return Gascony, but on terms beneficial to himself. In more leisurely moments Corbett had studied some of the memoranda and documents written by Philip IV's clever lawyers, particularly the writer, Pierre Dubois, who saw Philip as a new Charlemagne in Europe. Dubois recommended that Philip extend his power through a series of judicious marriage alliances. The French King seemed to agree with this, marrying his three sons to members of the powerful French nobility in the hope of annexing the independent Duchy of Burgundy.

On his journey to Dover and during the peaceful sea voyage Corbett had reached the conclusion that Philip would offer such a treaty to Edward. The English King's son was now six or seven years old and already there were rumours that Edward was looking for a bride amongst the powerful dukes in the Low Countries. Someone he could bring into his own circle of allies against Philip.

Philip would counter this: his wife, Joan of Navarre, had recently given birth to a young princess named Isabella. Corbett wondered if Philip intended to return Gascony on condition that Edward marry his heir to the young Princess Isabella? The more the clerk thought about such a plan, the more feasible it became and he only hoped that he would negotiate as skilfully as possible and not incur the anger of his ever irrational royal master.

Corbett had other instuctions. He was to continue to seek out the traitor on Edward's council. He considered the information he had garnered and believed Lancaster and the King would not disagree with it. Although Waterton was guilty of suspicious activities, he was not the traitor they were hunting. Corbett turned the matter over and over again in his mind, half-listening to Ranulf's grumbles about the French, the lack of food and the hostile company.

Corbett still missed Maeve, still loved her yet he felt a quiet surge of excitement over his present task; the traitor, whoever he or she might be, must surely become over confident? In all his previous investigations Corbett had discovered it was at such a moment that the culprit could be detected and brought to justice. As the envoys left Boulogne and began the long journey to Paris, Corbett felt that stage was fast approaching.

The journey was pleasant enough. A glorious summer and a golden sun had turned the barren Norman countryside into a vision of loveliness. Elm, sycamore, oak trees, majestic in their summer growth, the orchards and cornfields, full and ripe for the reaping. The prospect of a good harvest and an easy winter had relaxed the attitudes of the usually hostile peasants and taciturn manor lords, and they were shown hospitality at every place they stopped. Of course, Corbett attempted to open conversation with the French but he sensed de Craon's deep distrust of him which was reflected in the eyes of the rest of the French escort, even the elderly Count Louis of Evreux, whenever Corbett spoke they were watchful, suspicious, almost respectful as if they feared Corbett as animals might a skilled hunter.

Eight days after they had left Boulogne, they entered Paris, now a seething mass of people as the late summer fairs began. The streets were thronged with beggars, tinkers, pedlars, men and women of various nationalities, merchants who had drifted south from the Rhine or Low Countries in the hope of selling and buying goods. Even the execution ground, Montfaucon, was deserted despite the bodies swinging from a makeshift scaffold and the poor wretches locked in the stocks. Corbett and the French envoys crossed the River Seine, went through a maze of winding streets, past Notre Dame Cathedral and into the Louvre Palace.

Corbett paid his respects to Evreux and de Craon and, after receiving little thanks, was led off by a chamberlain, Ranulf and Hervey in his wake, to their quarters, three small garrets at the top of the palace. Corbett swore they were under the very eaves. Ranulf squeaked in protest and urged Corbett to remonstrate with Philip's chamberlain but the clerk, on reflection, thought differently. He was an envoy, but not in the usual sense, and the French would only delight in a fresh opportunity of provoking him. They were masters of protocol and courtly etiquette and Corbett sensed that he had been given this dingy garret and tawdry furniture in the hope of inciting him to some surprising outburst.

Moreover, the rooms were on one floor and Corbett knew he could come and go as he wished and be able to give the slip to the usual spies de Craon would feel obliged to send his way. Corbett instructed Ranulf and Hervey that on no account were they to leave the royal palace and to report to him immediately any suspicious occurrences or happenings. Hervey looked relieved at this but Ranulf sulked for hours when he realised he had been refused permission to run wild in the fleshpots of the city. The brothels and bordellos of Paris were famous for their whores, Ranulf had tasted some of these delights on his last visit and was disappointed to learn he would not be able to renew old acquaintances.

They settled down to the court routine, Corbett realising that the French would only receive him in an official audience when the time was ripe. They drew food from the buttery and kitchens, sometimes dining in the great hall beneath the silken canopies and arras bearing the White Cross of Lorraine or the Silver Fleur de Lis of France. Corbett constantly tried to learn what was going on; items of gossip, pieces of information, snatches of news which could be sewn together to form a mental tapestry.

He soon accepted this would be harder than he thought, de Craon or perhaps someone even higher, had issued the strictest instructions; the English envoys were to be treated kindly, afforded some hospitality but to be given no concessions and certainly not any gossip. Corbett found his witticisms and attempts at intelligent conversation rapidly brought to nothing, while even Ranulf's quick and easy tongue, subtle flatteries and droll humour made little headway with the serving girls who worked in the palace.

They also knew they were observed, which reduced Hervey to such constant agitation and nervous tension that Corbett tired of trying to allay his fears. Despite the colour, the pageantry, the glorious gaudy costumes of the household knights and the different ranks of servants, there was a sense of malice, of quiet menace in the palace. Corbett knew this atmosphere was not caused by de Craon but came direct from Philip, a king who prided himself on knowing every turn, every occurrence in his realm.

The days dragged on. Corbett spent most of his time either listening to the choirs in the royal chapel or browsing greedily amongst the rare books and manuscripts of the palace library. King Philip prided himself on being a man of culture and Corbett was delighted to find that royal French gold had purchased works of Aristotle from the Islamic writers of Spain and North Africa. His pleasure was marred by having to keep an ever-vigilant eye on Ranulf whose restless roaming about the palace could pose a threat to their security. Corbett knew that they were safe as long as they obeyed the strict protocol of the envoys. If that was broken, the French would rightly claim that they had usurped their rights and were subject to any punishment the French King thought fit.

One day, about a week after their arrival, Ranulf returned breathlessly to their garret to announce that he had discovered other English people in the palace. At first, Corbett thought he was mad, dismissing his words as mere fantasies, the result of too much wine or enforced loneliness. Yet, as Ranulf described what he had seen, Corbett sensed his servant was speaking the truth and had probably met some of the hostages Philip had demanded after the English army surrendered in Gascony. He decided that perhaps these were worth a visit and Ranulf gladly took him back. They were all in one of the small herb gardens which lay at the back of the palace, a fairly unprepossessing group of elderly men, women and a few children.

Corbett remembered the letters he had brought and was pleased to hear they had received them. He chatted for a while, giving them news of England and the royal court, trying to do his best to allay their anxieties and reassure them that their homesickness would soon be at an end. He met Tuberville's sons, two sturdy boys of eleven and thirteen who resembled their father as closely as peas out of a pod. Corbett found their youthful enthusiasm and constant questions about their father and home as a welcome relief to the gloom and despondency of the other hostages. They spoke of the letters they had received and the eldest, Jocelyn, openly confessed that sometimes he did not know what his father was writing about. Corbett laughed, promising to tell their father to write in a more clear and lucid fashion.

He was about to leave when he caught a glimpse of blond hair. He turned to gaze closer and his jaw fell open in surprise as he recognised the young woman he had last seen with de Craon and Waterton in that dingy Paris tavern so many weeks before.

'Who is that lady?' Corbett asked one of Tuberville's sons.

'Oh,' the boy replied scornfully, 'The Lady Eleanor, the Earl of Richmond's daughter. She keeps to herself and pines away in corners. She hardly ever talks to anyone.'

'Well,' Corbett murmured almost to himself, 'She is one person who is going to talk to me.'

He walked round one of the raised flower beds and approached the young woman, tapping her on the shoulder. She spun round, her blond hair swinging like a veil round her face. She was thin, pale, but her light blue eyes and perfectly formed features made her beautiful.

'What is it, Monsieur?' she asked.

'My lady,' Corbett replied. 'May I present my compliments. I am Hugh Corbett, senior clerk in the chancery of Edward of England. I am here on diplomatic business and also to present the compliments of your father as well as your secret admirer, Ralph Waterton.'

Of course it was all a lie but Corbett knew he had struck the truth, she blushed whilst her reply ended in an almost meaningless stammer.

'Ralph Waterton,' Corbett continued, 'is your secret admirer, is he not, my lady?'

'Yes,' she whispered.

'And you were sent by your father as hostage to France? To keep you out of Waterton's way?'

The young woman nodded.

'It was to keep you both apart,' Corbett continued relentlessly, 'that your father had Waterton transferred to the royal service. It was both a ruse and a bribe was it not?'

'Yes,' Lady Eleanor whispered, her eyes downcast, 'we

love each other deeply. My father was furious that I even looked at such a man.

'First, he threatened Ralph and then attempted to bribe him by recommending him to the King.'

'Did this work?'

The Lady Eleanor played nervously with the rings on her long white fingers.

'No,' she answered hoarsely, 'we continued to meet each other. My father threatened Ralph, who in turn replied that he would appeal direct to the King.'

'So,' Corbett interrupted brusquely, 'when your father had to send a hostage to France, he chose you? I also gather,' he continued, 'that Monsieur de Craon found out about your affair, or should I say liaison, and when Waterton came to Paris, he arranged secret meetings between you did he not?'

'Yes. Yes,' Lady Eleanor replied. 'Monsieur de Craon was most kind.'

'What price did de Craon ask?'

The young woman looked up in alarm and Crobett saw fear in her eyes and the slight tremble of her shoulders.

'There was no price,' she snapped back, 'Ralph is a loyal servant of the King. Monsieur de Craon did not even ask.'

'Then why did Monsieur de Craon extend such kindness to both of you?'

'I do not know,' Lady Eleanor replied, hiding her nervousness behind an assumed air of haughtiness, 'If you wish to know, why not ask him.'

And, without further ado, the lady spun on her heel and walked quickly away.

Corbett watched her go. His questions had sprung from a wild guess but the surmise had proved correct. Another missing piece was placed in the puzzle. Ends were matched. Slowly but surely the picture was emerging. De Craon had used both Waterton and the Lady Eleanor, but for what purpose? And if he was so concerned about the young lovers why had he not informed Lady Eleanor about Waterton's imprisonment? De Craon must surely know about that. The only reason could be that de Craon did not want to alarm the Lady Eleanor and Corbett was now fully aware of the logic behind that. Corbett sighed and walked slowly back into the palace buildings. He must be careful; if Lady Eleanor informed de Craon about what Corbett knew, envoy or not, Corbett would be far too dangerous to be allowed a safe passage back to England.

SEVENTEEN

Three days later Corbett was summoned to a meeting of Philip IV's council, held in the great hall of the palace; every care and attention had been taken to transform the place into a majestic and regal setting. Huge cloths of gold had been draped over rafter beams, pure white velvet arras hung from the walls depicting the insignia of Philip's famous and sainted ancestor Louis IX.

On the dais a row of chairs had been placed, each draped in a silver cloth except for the large central throne covered in purple velvet fringed with gold. Before this was a low stool and Corbett had no illusions about who was to sit there. The hall filled with various officials, men in the different striped robes of Philip's household, black and white, red and gold, green and black: household knights in silver-plated Milanese armour took up position around the hall, their drawn swords placed point down between their mailed feet, hands resting on the jewelled cross-hilts. Heralds in the gallery above the dais flourished their trumpets and a shrill, braying blast silenced the clamour of the hall. A side door opened, two thurifers, dressed in white robes with gold girdles round their waists, entered, their slowly swaying censers sending puffs of fragrant incense up into the hall. They took up positions at either end of the dais as the heralds followed, each bearing huge banners. Corbett only had eyes for the one carrying the Oriflamme, the sacred pennant of the Capetian kings usually kept behind the high altar in the royal chapel of St. Denis.

The heralds were followed by members of Philip's family, sons, brothers and cousins, all resplendent in purple and gold. There was a pause, silence and then the trumpets brayed another long thrilling blast and Philip entered, brilliant in cloth of gold, his gown fringed with the costliest lambswool. A pair of golden spurs clanked on his black leather riding-boots which peered incongruously from beneath the long court gown. Corbett smiled to himself. Philip IV was a master of protocol and court ceremony but, even here, he could not hide his great love of hunting. Corbett suspected that the King had recently returned from one of his hunting lodges in either the Bois de Boulogne or the forests of Vincennes.

Philip sat on the throne, his family and entourage also took their seats. De Craon appeared as if from nowhere and beckoned Corbett and his party forward to the stools, Ranulf and Hervey sat down, overawed and open-mouthed at the gorgeous panoply of splendid power around them. Corbett slowly took his seat, carefully arranging his robe, taking time with all his movements before schooling his features to become the experienced diplomat prepared to receive messages on behalf of his royal master.

He stared at Philip but the French king's face was impassive as carved alabaster, though Corbett was quietly pleased to see a flicker of annoyance cross de Craon's face. Clerks scurried about, documents were unrolled and once more Corbett had to listen to the Process of Gascony, a long list of French grievances over the duchy. He had heard it before and sat half-listening as the clerk droned on, only becoming attentive when the clerk paused to intone a new passage, '*Autem nunc Regi Franciae placet*', 'However it now pleases the King of France'.

Corbett listened carefully, trying to control his excitement as the clerk began to unfold Philip's offer of peace. The French king was prepared to submit all grievances to His Holiness, Pope Boniface VIII – Philip's creature Corbett thought: the French would restore the duchy in the hope that Edward would agree to a marriage between the Prince of Wales and Philip's daughter, Isabella, and that Gascony would eventually be ruled by one of their offspring. So, Corbett mused, he had been correct: Philip could not hold the duchy for ever but might restore it on a binding arbitration guaranteed by the Pope. At the same time he would limit Edward's own diplomacy whilst ensure that one grandson would sit on the throne of England while another ruled Gascony.

The clerk stopped talking. Corbett was aware that the French, including Philip, were staring at him, awaiting his reply but he had already decided, Lancaster had given him one instruction:

'Agree to anything, anything which will give us time. Once we have the duchy, we can think again about Philip's terms.'

Corbett cleared his throat.

'*Placet*,' he stated, '*Hic Regi Angliae placebit* – this pleases, will please the King of England.' Corbett sensed the deep relief of the French. Philip almost smiled, his entourage visibly relaxed, while de Craon's glee was more than apparent. Corbett shifted uneasily: he had overlooked one thing: as long as Philip's traitor was on Edward's council, the French would always know of any attempt by Edward to subvert or ignore the terms of the arbitration.

Nevertheless, it was too late now: Philip rose, the

meeting was at an end. De Craon left the dais and walked over to Corbett, he made little attempt to hide his pleasure over the proposed settlement. The Frenchman nodded benevolently at Ranulf and Hervey before turning to Corbett.

'Well, Monsieur. You think your King will accept these terms?'

'There is little reason to doubt he will,' Corbett replied as non-committal as possible.

De Craon rubbed his chin and smiled.

'Good. Good.' He was about to turn away when suddenly, almost as an afterthought, he spun round. 'His Grace, the King is holding a banquet here tonight. He would like you,' he smiled expansively at Ranulf and Hervey, 'all of you to be his guests. Till then, adieu.'

He sauntered off as if his every problem had been resolved. Corbett watched him go, trying to suppress the fury welling up inside him, making his heart pound harder and his throat constrict, Hervey expressed mild enjoyment at such a gracious invitation and recoiled in horror at the anger which blazed in Corbett's face.

By the time Corbett and his party returned to the palace that same evening, the clerk's temper had cooled. He had accepted Philip's proposals on Edward's behalf but the English king was only vulnerable if the spy was allowed to remain free. Corbett now accepted that Waterton was not the traitor and hoped the over-confidence of the French would provide some sign, some clue about whom they had bought on Edward's council.

The French were certainly determined to show the full splendour of their power. The great hall shimmered in silks, velvet, multi-coloured tapestries: the tables were covered in white lawn fringed with gold. Silver plates, diamond-encrusted cups and gold flagons gleamed and winked in the light of thousands of beeswax candles in huge bronze candelabra placed in rows along the hall. Philip and his family, resplendent in purples, whites and golds, sat at the high table almost hidden by a huge pure gold salt cellar. In the gallery musicians with rebec, flute, tambour and viol competed desperately with the growing clamour as the wine circulated and servants brought in course after course of lampreys, eels, salmon, venison garnished with tangy spices, a huge swan cooked and dressed, it seemed to swim on the great silver serving plate. Corbett and his party sat at a table just beneath the great dais, de Craon opposite them a smile on his face as he stared directly across at Corbett.

The English clerk did not relish the enjoyment on his opponent's face and sat there, moodily playing with his food and sipping gently from his cup. Beside him, however, Ranulf and Hervey were eating like men who had been starved of food for months. De Craon watched them. His supercilious smile infuriated Corbett but the clerk had enough sense to realise that any outburst would only increase the Frenchman's enjoyment. It was evident that de Craon believed that he and Philip had achieved a diplomatic *coup*. Edward's heir would be married to Philip's daughter. Philip's grandson would one day sit on the English throne and, if Edward made any secret attempts to outflank the French manoeuvres, their spy on the English council would promptly inform them and to be forewarned was to be forearmed. Corbett pushed his plate away and rested his elbows on the table.

'Monsieur,' he said softly, 'You must be very pleased by today's events.'

De Craon idly picked his teeth with his finger, totally ignoring the look of disgust on Corbett's face.

'Of course, Monsieur,' he said slowly, at the same time dislodging a piece of chewed meat from his teeth which he looked at before popping it back into his mouth. 'We do not see it as a victory,' he continued, 'but merely the restoration of Philip's rights in France and in Europe as a whole.'

'And the hostages?' Corbett said carefully; 'They will be returned?'

De Craon smirked. 'Of course. Once the processes have been sealed formally by your master, we will ship them home as quickly as possible. They are a burden on the royal expenses.'

'All of them?' Corbett sharply enquired. The smile on de Craon's face vanished.

'What do you mean?' he asked suspiciously.

'Does that include the Earl of Richmond's daughter?'

'Of course.'

Corbett nodded. 'Good! And Tuberville's sons?'

'Of course,' de Craon snapped.

The French clerk sipped slowly from his flagon. Corbett had watched him throughout the meal and realised that the Frenchman had drunk often and deep. His face was now flushed, his eyes glittering, a mixture of self-satisfaction and rich red Bordeaux.

'Tuberville's sons,' de Craon continued expansively, 'will go home. That poor father and his letters which tell them all the details about St. Christopher medals and life in some rugged little manor house in Shropshire would touch the heart of any man. Naturally, the Earl of Richmond's daughter will be the first to go. Our King will insist on that.'

Corbett nodded understandingly though he could hardly believe his good fortune. He schooled his features, continuing to look as if he was miserable and deeply unhappy for, if de Craon sensed he had been trapped, then Corbett would not be allowed to leave France alive. Corbett put his cup down, yawned and turned to Ranulf.

'We should be gone,' he said quietly. Ranulf, his mouth full of rich food, nodded and promptly began to fill his pockets with the sweet pastry which the chef had laid on the table before him. Hervey was almost asleep he had drunk so much and Corbett had to shake him roughly awake. De Craon leaned across the table.

'You are going now, Monsieur?'

'Of course,' Crobett replied. 'In fact, I would like to leave for London tomorrow.'

De Craon's eyes narrowed. 'Why? Why the haste?'

Corbett shrugged. 'Why not. We have your master's terms. They are not to be written down but to be conveyed verbally to Edward of England. There is no reason for us to stay. Besides, there are matters in London which require my attention.'

De Craon nodded slowly. His eyes searched Corbett's face as if trying to find any reason why the clerk had decided to leave so quickly.

'You are sure, Monsieur?'

'Of course,' Crobett replied, still acting the role of the depressed diplomat. 'These terms are not advantageous to Edward. The sooner we return to England and inform his Grace, the better. I would be obliged, Monsieur, if you would arrange for the safe conducts to be given to us with a suitable military escort to take us to Calais.'

De Craon shrugged. He knew he could not keep this English clerk if he wished to return. But de Craon was suspicious. Had Corbett discovered something? He wanted this English clerk to make a mistake, just one and so de Craon could revenge himself for previous insults inflicted by this insufferable Englishman. Nor had de Craon forgotten that Corbett was responsible for the recent death of one of his best agents. The Frenchman tried to clear the intoxicating fumes from his head as he concentrated on what he had said to

Corbett since the Englishman had arrived in Paris. There was nothing. Nothing had been given away. De Craon rose.

'Your safe conducts will be ready tomorrow morning. I wish you a safe journey,' and, having said this, he spun on his heel and walked up to the high table to whisper softly in the ear of his royal master. Corbett did not bother to see if Philip objected but, half dragging Hervey and pushing Ranulf, left the hall for their chambers.

EIGHTEEN

De Craon was true to his word, the warrants were ready, as was a small military escort hand-picked by de Craon himself.

Throughout their journey across the early autumn Norman countryside Corbett was careful to keep his thoughts to himself and continue to act as if he was the bearer of bad news. Ranulf and Hervey were delighted to be returning to England but Ranulf knew enough about his master's moods to remain silent and not try to vex him with idle chatter. The captain of the escort, a burly Breton, watched the English envoy carefully, being secretly instructed to do so by de Craon himself. De Craon believed that Corbett knew something but could not fathom what it was. However, throughout the journey, the clerk's sad demeanour and apparent agitation made the escort relax and at Boulogne the captain sent a courier back to de Craon with a verbal message that the English envoy continued to behave as if he dreaded the coming meeting with his royal master in England. They were put aboard a merchant cog bound for Dover and from there Corbett was able to secure horses to travel to London.

If his journey back had been quiet and uneventful, the subsequent interview with Edward of England was a stark contrast. Hervey and Ranulf were not allowed into the royal chamber but Corbett attended the meeting, grateful at least that the King had decided to have Edmund of Lancaster also present. Edward heard Corbett out, before bursting into one of his famous royal rages. Tables and stools were overturned, manuscripts thrown and rushes kicked as Edward stormed around the room calling Philip of France every filthy name Corbett knew and a few he did not.

'That man,' Edward roared, 'is a danger to Europe and threatens our very crown. He would like his own misbegotten grandson on my throne! He intends to build an empire which rivals Caesar's or even Charlemagne's, but he will not.' The King's rage lasted for an hour before he eventually calmed down.

He drank deeply from a wine bowl before crossing to Corbett and bringing both of his jewelled-bedecked hands slapping down on the clerk's shoulders. Corbett stared into his blue red-flecked eyes.

'Corbett,' the King rasped, 'You are the bearer of very bad news. I understand that in ancient times such a messenger would be promptly executed. I am almost tempted to carry that out myself. At other times and on other occasions I couldn't carc what Philip intends to do for his blessed daughter but you know, Master Clerk, that any attempt we make to break free from the Pope's arbitration would be immediately reported to Philip by the spy or spies who now sit at our very council.' The King pushed his face close to Corbett, who stared back unflinchingly. 'You have come home,' the King said, 'not only bearing these bad tidings but with your guess, your reasonable deductions, that Waterton is not the spy.'

Corbett controlled the panic he felt and coolly stared back at the King.

'Your Grace,' he replied, 'I have always served you, your crown, your family. I went to France with careful instructions given to me by your brother,' he turned and nodded to where Lancaster slouched anxiously against a wall, 'I had no choice but to accept Philip's terms. It is one way you will have the duchy returned.'

'It is one way I get the duchy returned!' Edward mimicked, 'For God's sake, Corbett, don't you realise that as long as a spy is on our council any secret we discuss, any attempt to outmanoeuvre Philip, will be brought to nothing.'

Corbett cleared his throat and chose his words carefully. 'I cannot,' he began, grateful that the King had now removed his hands from his shoulders and walked back to sit on a chair. 'I cannot,' he repeated, 'allow Waterton to go to the scaffold. I believe he is a love-sick, rather stupid young man, but not a traitor. However, your Grace, before you pass judgement on me I do have other news but I must have your word that you do not challenge or question me.'

Edward accepted that with an airy wave of his hand. Corbett paused. 'I know who the traitor is!' he announced. Edward shot up in his chair as if struck by a blow while the look on Lancaster's face was one of pure astonishment.

'Who is he, Corbett?' the King asked quietly. 'Who is the misbeggoten cur?'

'I know,' Corbett replied coolly, 'but I cannot give you the name. You must give me time, your Grace. I need evidence and I know where to look.'

The King rose and walked slowly over to Corbett. 'I promise you, Hugh,' he said, 'that if you deliver this man, you may ask for anything in my kingdom and it will be yours. You have a week.'

Corbett bowed and left the chamber. Once the door had closed behind him he leaned against the cold brickwork as he tried to control the trembling of his own body while fervently hoping that he could keep his promise to the King.

The next day Corbett returned to the Palace of Westminster. Through Lancaster's intercession Waterton was freed from the Tower, bathed, dressed, given a filling meal but kept under close guarded secrecy in a chamber in Westminster Palace well away from any prying eyes. Corbett visited him, placating the clerk's hostility by pointing out that it was he who had managed to secure his release. He questioned Waterton very carefully about the council meetings, the procedures, who was present and, above all, what happened after the council meetings ended. It took some time. Waterton, like any clerk, attempted to dismiss the minor matters but Corbett knew these very petty details would provide the evidence to arrest the traitor.

After much questioning, probing, even a heated row, Corbett managed to confirm the suspicions he had formed in France, so he asked the chief clerk of the Chancery for copies of all letters and records sent to France, both to the royal court as well as to the hostages. Over the next few days Corbett studied these, hardly leaving the chamber except to drink, eat or relieve himself. It took some time but, eventually, he had the evidence he needed and Corbett immediately demanded an audience with the King.

At Corbett's request Edward agreed to meet him in one of the rose gardens behind the Palace of Westminster, a small enclosure, the walls of the palace rising up on every side. Corbett usually loved the place with the roses in full bloom in their raised flower beds interspersed with small patches of herbs which, when crushed, gave off a fragrant smell but the King took one look at Corbett's face and realised that the clerk was blind to his surroundings and Edward was too cunning to push or try such a man's patience. Corbett was unshaven, his eyes red from lack of sleep, his garments stained due to hasty meals and a lack of time to bathe or even change. Edward gestured him to sit on one of the walls of the raised flower bed and sat alongside, almost as if they were two old friends rather than a king and a faithful retainer. Corbett asked the King to remain silent while he went through all the evidence he had collected and Edward did so, head bowed, hands in his lap, he listened like a priest hearing the confession of a man who had not been shriven for years.

Corbett talked quietly but remorselessly, building up a picture of what had happened to Edward's army in Gascony and tracing all the developments since. The loss of English spies in Paris, the destruction of the ship *St. Christopher*, his own adventures there, his suspicions and why he had eventually decided that this particular person was the traitor. He produced evidence, sheet after sheet of vellum with carefully written conclusions which Edward studied. When Corbett finally finished, the King, head in hands, could hardly believe it.

Corbett watched him nervously. Edward was a strange man, on the one hand, hard, ruthless, he would without any compunction, order men, women and even children to be slain in a town which had resisted him. On the other, he was almost like a child, if he trusted someone he expected that trust to be returned and could never understand why people broke their word. The person Corbett named had not only broken the oath of fealty and loyalty but friendship and trust as well.

Edward asked one question. 'Are you certain, Corbett?' and the clerk answered it with his own.

'Are you sure, your Grace?'

The King nodded. 'I am,' he replied quietly. 'He is undoubtedly a traitor. Any court in Christendom would accept the evidence you have offered and sent him immediately to the scaffold. If it is to be done,' a note of hardness crept into the King's voice, 'then it had best be done quickly.' He called out and a retainer appeared at a small doorway which led into the palace. He came across to the King who whispered a few instructions into the man's ear. The man looked startled, but Edward repeated them fiercely. The retainer nodded and walked quickly away.

While they waited the King just sat staring moodily into the distance as Corbett, for the final time, went over in his own mind the evidence he had acquired. The King was right, the man was a traitor and deserved to die but he still dreaded the coming meeting. Sir Thomas Tuberville stepped into the garden and the King beckoned him over to sit on the wall opposite him.

'Sir Thomas,' the King began, 'You are to arrrest the traitor.'

Tuberville looked surprised. 'I thought we already had, your Grace. Waterton, the clerk, he is in the Tower.'

'No! No!' the King answered. 'Waterton has been released. He is no more a traitor than Corbett here.'

'Then who?'

Corbett watched Tuberville's eyes narrow and the colour leave his face. Edward simply stretched out his hand and tapped Tuberville gently on the leg.

'You know who, Sir Thomas. Yourself! You are the traitor!'

Tuberville immediately sprang to his feet, his hand flying to the sword which hung from his belt.

'Sir Thomas,' the King said, 'Do not do that. If you look up at the windows surrounding the garden you will notice that there are royal crossbow men placed at every one. They have orders to shoot you, not to kill you, but wound you in the arm or leg and I promise you that will only be the beginning of your agonies.'

Tuberville looked up and so did Corbett. The King

was right. At every window, at every opening, they could see the glimpse of metal and a dash of colour, each representing a trained crossbow man, their evil weapons aiming directly down at Tuberville.

Tuberville slouched back on the wall and Corbett almost felt sorry for him. A sheen of sweat had appeared on the man's pale face and the knight was doing his best to stop his body from trembling.

'You have no evidence!' he said hoarsely. 'I served you, your Grace, well in Gascony. You know that.'

'We have every proof,' the King replied. 'Corbett has collected it.'

The clerk flinched at the look of pure hatred which Tuberville sent him.

'I knew you were a dangerous man, Corbett,' he rasped. 'But not this dangerous. If you think I am the traitor, then you must have the evidence, so why not tell me?'

'It's quite simple,' Corbett replied. 'I don't know why you became a traitor, Sir Thomas, but I know how. After you returned from Gascony you made a secret pact with Philip and the French court to supply information to them. The French knew that you were a knight of the royal household and were privy to secrets. They probably increased their demands when they knew that you were appointed to the post of the captain of the guard which protected the royal council chamber.'

'Exactly!' Tuberville exclaimed triumphantly. 'I was to guard the chamber, not be in it and listen to the King and his councillors discuss secret matters!'

'Ah,' Corbett answered, 'but when the council was over, Sir Thomas, it was you who tidied the council room up. Scraps of paper, memoranda, you even helped Waterton file and put them away and, of course, Waterton, with other things on his mind, was only too willing to allow you to finish these matters while he escaped from the palace and the possible enmity of the Earl of Richmond. Because,' Corbett continued remorselessly, 'you knew Waterton's secret. You became friends. He told you about his love for the Earl's daughter and the Earl's hostility towards him. You offered to protect him. When a council meeting was over and the minutes had been written and redrafted, it was Waterton's duty to write them out fully. You made sure that you were always there. After all,' Corbett remarked, 'why should Waterton be suspicious? In Gascony you had proved yourself to be one of the King's most able commanders, the only man who had attempted to break out of the French trap. You had a lot in common, a mutual hatred of Richmond which opened the door to royal secrets. Waterton did commit a crime but it was one of carelessness not malice.'

Corbett watched Tuberville's face and saw the tension in the man's eyes prove that he was correct.

'Tell him, Corbett,' the King began, 'Tell him how he sent the information to France.'

'Shall I tell you, Sir Thomas?' Corbett said, suddenly hating this man who had sent his friends and other Englishmen to cruel, unexpected deaths. 'You used your sons, the letters you wrote to them. They were cleverly written. They bore messages for your new French masters. When I visited your children in Paris they commented on how sometimes they could not understand the references you were making. I thought this when I first saw them. Full of strange comments, places and names, but there again, at the time, I thought this was simply a result of grief. However, de Craon proved that your letters were not a simple collection of pieces of advice and news. First, he seemed to remember the content of your letters very well. Rather strange, one of Philip's principal ministers should remember details of a letter an English knight had written some months ago to one of his young children in France.' Corbett paused and licked his lips, but hurried on before Tuberville could interrupt. 'So, when I came back to England, I studied one of your letters.' Corbett dug into his pouch and brought out a small piece of parchment. 'One sentence reads "*the ship which sails from Bordeaux bringing me home to England from you*". The next sentence begins "*On October fourteenth I intend to go back to the Welsh march.*" The third sentence begins "*The Saint Christopher which I have given you*".' Corbett pauses and throws a look at Tuberville, whose face was now white with terror. 'And, finally, the next sentence begins "*A dangerous occasion might arise*".'

Corbett thrusts the piece of parchment into Tuberville's hands. 'The sentences are quite erratic,' the clerk continued. 'They give jumbled pieces of information. However, take the opening words of each sentence and you suddenly have your message to the French: that the ship called Saint Christopher is leaving Bordeaux on fourteenth October and because of that a dangerous occasion might arise. De Craon is not the most intelligent of men but the message was quite simple. The *Saint Christopher* was carrying messages to our King which might prove dangerous to the French. You passed this information on and the *Saint Christopher* was stopped and sunk with a loss of all hands. The King lost a ship as well as valuable information about his enemies abroad.'

Corbett threw the piece of parchment at Tuberville. 'You can go through others of your letters and they bear similar messages. You talk about travelling through Flanders yet you never intended to go there. Later, in the same letter, you actually refer to a friend called Aspale but no such friend exists. What you were doing was informing de Craon about a clerk, Robert Aspale, who has been sent to France to spy on our behalf.' Corbett stood up.

'You killed my friend, you killed others, you are a traitor and you deserve to die!'

Tuberville looked down at his hands which lay clenched in his lap. 'Is there any more?' he said.

'Oh, yes,' Corbett replied heatedly. 'There is more! I do not know what instructions the French gave you regarding Scotland but you were certainly in correspondence with that misbegotten rebel, the Lord Morgan! The King constantly sent messengers there insisting that the Lord Morgan keep his peace. You just ensured that you prepared the horse, using a special saddle, one with a secret cavity for your own treasonable messages. Waterton thought that was strange. The King's spy in Wales discovered this and so Morgan killed him. Now,' Corbett concluded drily, 'Do we have the evidence? As the King said,' and the clerk looked down where the King sat on the garden wall, 'The evidence we have will be acceptable before any court, English or French. You are the traitor! And for what? A bag of gold?'

'No!' Tuberville's head suddenly shot up, his eyes glaring at both Corbett and the King. 'Not gold!' He too rose, chest heaving to confront Corbett. 'I am not a traitor! I fought for the King in Gascony! I served him here at home but that misbegotten noble, the Earl of Richmond, he spoilt it all. He lost the army, he lost the province, he lost our honour and he had the impunity to accuse me of being rash, whereas his laziness and insolence were the biggest treasons of all. Because of him I was captured and led like some fool through the streets while the French laughed. Because of him I had to send my own children to France as hostages, and on my return to England Richmond scarcely punished, hardly reprimanded!' Tuberville glared down at the King. 'I believe you lost your own honour. Richmond should have died for what happened in Gascony!' Tuberville sat down again. 'While I was in Paris, de

Craon visited me. He praised my courage in attempting to break out of the French encircling force. He also said my children would be sent to France as hostages but added he would take great care of them.

'Indeed, he made further promises about giving me lands and a manor house and being able to join them there, so I accepted. De Craon told me to garner any information I knew about the English troops on the south coast, or the King's intentions with regard to Gascony. When de Craon heard that I had been made captain of the guard protecting the royal council chamber, his promises were all the more lavish, that once Philip's terms had been accepted by Edward, I and my children would be created nobles in France and given extensive lands where I could begin a new life.'

'The only thing you will begin,' the King interrupted harshly, 'is a sentence of imprisonment which will lead to a trial for high treason and execution according to the form and due process of law!' Edward's raised voice brought a group of soldiers into the garden. The King looked up. 'I trusted you, Sir Thomas, I advanced your career. I would have looked after you. Richmond has been punished for his incompetence in France, but I always draw a line between mistakes and malice, between carelessness and treason. You are a traitor, Sir Thomas, and will suffer the full rigours of the law!'

Tuberville just shrugged, cast a look of hatred towards Corbett and, without making further resistance, allowed himself to be marched away.

'What will happen to him?' Corbett asked.

'He will stand trial,' the King replied, 'Before his peers and my judges at Westminster Hall. The evidence you have accumulated will send him to the execution block. He will be hanged, drawn and quartered. A warning to any other person who even thinks of committing treason in my realm! Waterton alone will demand that,' the King added bitterly. 'It was clever, very clever of de Craon to arrange events to throw the blame on him.' He looked sharply at Corbett. 'Were you always convinced that Waterton was innocent?'

'Yes, yes, I think I was,' the clerk replied slowly. 'Something in my heart which became clearer when I met Richmond's daughter in Paris but, really, de Craon told me. I watched his face that day in the great council chamber when your brother announced that we had discovered and arrested the traitor. I saw the flicker of delight in de Craon's face and eyes. He must have known we had arrested the wrong man and so he betrayed himself. During Lancaster's embassy to France,' Corbett continued, 'de Craon deliberately misled me. He favoured Waterton so as to arouse our suspicions.'

'But de Craon tried to kill you in Paris.'

'Just to throw suspicion on Waterton, the same applies to the French seal left in our diplomatic pouches. It was put there by de Craon, who also fed similar lies to his Scottish allies in the hope they would be passed on to you.'

The King nodded and stared at a rose in full bloom. He could scarcely believe what he had heard and seen. Tuberville a traitor! And such a devious one. God knows, the King thought, what a proper study of his letters would reveal. No wonder the Scottish and Welsh rebels had been so arrogant in their defiance. Edward glared at the rose as he plotted his revenge.

Corbett broke the ensuing silence by going down on one knee in front of the King.

'Your Grace,' he said. 'You did promise me that if I found the traitor, I could ask for anything in your kingdom.'

Edward looked down slyly.

'I was angry then, Master Corbett. And it is wrong to

quote a prince's words back to him, words which were said in the heat of the moment.'

Corbett smiled wanly. 'And the psalmist says "Put not your trust in princes", your Grace. Is this an example of it?'

Edward laughed softly. 'No, no, Hugh. I keep my word.'

'Good,' Corbett said. 'There are two things I wish, your Grace. First, for Tuberville's punishment to be commuted, let him be executed, let him be hanged, not the drawing and the quartering, the dismembering of a man's body. Justice does not demand that.'

The King looked up at the blue sky. 'Your request is granted,' he replied sharply, 'There is something else?'

'Yes,' Corbett continued, 'The Lord Morgan in Wales.'

'The Lord Morgan in Wales,' Edward interrupted harshly 'has already felt my displeasure! I have moved troops down from Caernarvon and Caerphilly Castles. They are all over the Lord Morgan's estates as well as the surrounding countryside. I doubt if that Welshman will ever give me further trouble!'

'It's not the Lord Morgan,' Corbett interrupted rather abruptly, 'But his niece, the Lady Maeve.'

Edward looked sharply at Corbett before throwing his head back and guffawing with laughter.

'It is funny, Hugh,' he said, 'that you ask me about her, because we received a message from Lord Morgan along with one from his niece. Lord Morgan humbly submitted to our peace and begs for pardon for any mistakes or crimes he may have made. Of course, I will grant it after a while, but the Lady Maeve's message was much more simple. We were asked to give you this.'

The King dug into his purse and drew out the ring that Corbett had last seen in Maeve's hand, on the beach outside Neath Castle.

'She sent you this,' the King dropped the ring into Crobett's hand and smiled at the clerk's evident disappointment.

'Oh, there was a message, Master Clerk. The Lady Maeve wrote in support of her uncle's pleas for clemency, adding the postscript that she enclosed the ring for you in the hope that you would return it to her personally so that she could keep it for ever.'

Corbett just smiled, though his heart danced with joy. Still kneeling, he took the King's hand and kissed the ring.

'Do I have your permission, your Grace?'

'Of course,' the King said. 'Provided you are back in London for Tuberville's trial.'

* * *

It was a cold October morning, the palace yard at Westminster was packed to overflowing, the crowd pressing in around the great scaffold, as if they were all trying to draw warmth from the huge, black, iron brazier which burned there. Corbett was present, Ranulf beside him. All of London, the great lords and ladies in their silks and costly raiment. Corbett had come at the King's command. He did not like executions but felt he would have to see this matter through to the bitter end.

Tuberville had been tried before a special commission of gaol delivery. He had confessed to all his crimes and sentence had been pronounced by the Chief Justice, Roger de Brabazon, the principal judge of King's Bench. Edward, however, kept his word, the sentence being commuted to one of simple hanging. There were to be none of the terrible severities of disembowelling, burning, beheading and quartering suffered recently by Prince David of Wales.

After sentence Tuberville had been taken to the Tower and, early on this dark October morning, he had been brought back from the Tower to Westminster mounted on a poor hack, his feet bound under the horse's belly, his hands tied in front of him. Around him had ridden six tormentors dressed like devils. One of them held the hack's rein, another the halter in which Tuberville would hang whilst the rest baited and goaded their prisoner. Tuberville, dressed in full knightly regalia, had first been taken in to Westminster Hall to receive judgement and now, before sentence was carried out, he was to be degraded.

A scaffold had been erected just outside the main door of Westminster Hall, a raised stand where the judges sat and alongside them a rough post on which Tuberville's shield hung upside down, now smeared with black pitch and animal dung.

There was a blast from the trumpets. The doors opened and the heralds brought Tuberville out dressed in complete armour and wearing all the decorations of his knightly orders. Priests took up position on either side of the scaffold and began to intone the Vigil for the dead. As each psalm ended, the heralds stripped one piece of the prisoner's armour, beginning with his helmet, finally, the man was naked except for a loincloth. Tuberville's reversed shield was then taken down and broken into three pieces and a bowl of dirty water mixed with animal piss was emptied over Tuberville's head.

Once the ceremony was over, a loud sigh escaped from the throats of the crowd, rocks were hurled, abuse called, while the executioners took over. Tuberville was hustled to the gound and tied to a hurdle made out of ox hide. This was fastened to six horses who would drag it all the way from Westminster to the conduit in Cheapside and then back to the gallows, the Elms at Smithfield. Corbett was pleased that the King had not passed an act of attainder against Tuberville's family, consequently the traitor knight's sons would still be allowed to inherit their property and not suffer for the sins of their father. He was even more glad now as he watched Tuberville accept with quiet dignity all the insults and humiliations now heaped upon him. Tuberville was fastened onto the ox hide, his body already bruised and cut by the rocks thrown at him and Corbett closed his eyes as the hangman brought down his hand on the rump of one of the horses and the macabre procession, preceded by the tormentors, made its way down to the execution ground, the crowd surging after, shouting and laughing.

Corbett knew how it would end. He looked up at the darkening sky, the clouds scudding in over the Thames. Tuberville would be taken to the scaffold and there hanged until dead. His body would then be encased in chains and put in some public place as a warning to all who committed treason against the King. Corbett did not have enough malice inside him to watch the poor man's death agonies. Instead, he turned away and took joy in the thought that Maeve would soon be in London. Her uncle, the Lord Morgan, had to make his peace personally with the King. He had written to Edward saying that he would be in England by the Feast of All Saints, the beginning of November, Maeve would be with him. Corbett quietly said a 'Miserere' for Tuberville's soul which would soon be speeding its way to God. He also said a prayer for himself that perhaps Maeve might thaw the winter in his own heart.

AUTHOR'S NOTE

Perhaps the English can be excused if they believe that having double agents high in their government is only a phenomenon of the twentieth-century. Scandals regarding Philby, Burgess and Maclean, however, have their echoes in the treason of Thomas Tuberville, who was successfully managed by the French and was able to send information to them about the secret plans of the English king. We do know that Tuberville sent letters to the French – one is actually still extant in the Record Office in Chancery Lane, London. We also know that he was in treasonable correspondence with the Welsh rebel, Lord Morgan and aided Philip in building up his great alliance against Edward who was forced to accept the French King's terms.

The details of Tuberville's capture are shrouded in mystery but it was only achieved after a great deal of careful plotting and intrigue. He was captured and his treason exposed but not before he had caused terrible damage to the King's cause in Europe. However, unlike modern spies, Tuberville, rightly or wrongly, paid for his treason with his life.